MY SON THE FANATIC

MY SON
THE FANATIC
Hanif Kureishi

faber and faber

First published in 1997
by Faber and Faber Limited
3 Queen Square London WC1N 3AU

Photoset by Parker Typesetting Service, Leicester
Printed in England by Clays Ltd, St Ives plc

© Hanif Kureishi, 1997

Photographs by Joth Shakerley
© Zephyr Films, 1997

Hanif Kureishi is hereby identified as author of this
work in accordance with Section 77 of the Copyright,
Designs and Patents Act 1988

A CIP record for this book
is available from the British Library

ISBN 0–571–19234–3

2 4 6 8 10 9 7 5 3

CONTENTS

My Son The Fanatic was first shown as part of the Director's Fortnight at the 1997 Cannes Film Festival. The cast and crew includes:

PARVEZ	Om Puri
BETTINA	Rachel Griffiths
SCHITZ	Stellan Skarsgard
FARID	Akbar Kurtha
MINOO	Gopi Desai
FIZZY	Harish Patel
MAULVI	Bhasker Patel
Casting	Simone Ireland
	Vanessa Pereira
Make-Up Designer	Penny Smith
Costume Designer	Mary-Jane Reyner
Music Consultant	Charlie Gillett
Original Music	Stephen Warbeck
Line Producer	Anita Overland
Production Designer	Grenville Horner
Editor	David Gamble
Director of Photography	Alan Almond
Executive Producer	George Faber
Screenplay	Hanif Kureishi
	based on his short story
Producer	Chris Curling
Director	Udayan Prasad

A Zephyr Films Production

A BBC Films in association with UGC DA International & The Arts Council of England Presentation.

INTRODUCTION: THE ROAD EXACTLY

The idea for *My Son the Fanatic*, as for *The Black Album*, was provided by my thinking about the fatwah against Salman Rushdie, announced in February 1989. At that time various politicians, thinkers and artists spoke out in the media about this extraordinary intellectual terror. A surprising number of statements were fatuous and an excuse for abuse and prejudice; some expressed genuine outrage, and most were confused but comfortingly liberal. The attack on Rushdie certainly made people think afresh about the point and place of literature, about what stories were for, and about their relation to dissent.

But few commentators noticed that the objections to *The Satanic Verses* represented another kind of protest. In Britain many young Asians were turning to Islam, and some to a particularly extreme form, often called Fundamentalism. Most of these young people were from Muslim families, of course, but usually families in which the practice of religion, in a country to which their families had come to make a new life, had fallen into disuse.

It perplexed me that young people, brought up in secular Britain, would turn to a form of belief that denied them the pleasures of the society in which they lived. Islam was a particularly firm way of saying 'no' to all sorts of things. Young people's lives are, for a lot of the time, devoted to pleasure: the pleasure of sex and music, of clubbing, friendship, and the important pleasure of moving away from one's parents to develop one's own ideas. Why was it important that this group kept pleasure at a distance? Why did they wish to maintain such a tantalizing relation to their own enjoyment, keeping it so fervently in mind, only to deny it? Or was this puritanism a kind of rebellion, a brave refusal of the order of the age – an over-sexualized but sterile society? Were these young Muslims people who dared to try nothing? Whatever the reason, there was, clearly, a future in illusion; not only that, illusions were once more becoming a sound investment. But what sort of future did they require?

To the surprise of most of us, it sometimes seems that we are living in a new theocratic age. I imagined that the sixties, with its penchant for seeing through things, and pulling them apart with laughter and questions, had cleared that old church stuff away. But the sixties, in the West, with its whimsy and drugged credulity, also helped finish off the Enlightenment. It was during the sixties that weird cults, superstitious groups, new agers, strange therapists, seers, gurus and leaders of all kinds came to prominence. This need for belief and the establishment of new idols was often innocuous – a mixture of the American idea of self-fulfilment and the Greek notion of fully extended man, vitiated by a good dose of ordinary repression.

But the kind of religion favoured by the young Muslims was particularly strict and frequently authoritarian. An old religion was being put to a new use, and it was that use which interested me. I wondered constantly why people would wish to give so much of their own autonomy, the precious freedom of their own minds, to others – to Maulvis, and to the Koran. After all, the young people I met were not stupid; many were very intelligent. But they put a lot of effort into the fashioning of a retributive God to which to submit.

Clearly, where there is a 'crisis of authority', when, it seems, people aren't certain of anything because ancient hierarchies have been brought down, the answer is to create a particularly strict authority, where troubling questions cannot be admitted. 'There's too much freedom,' one of the young men, Ali, kept saying to me, someone who'd always thought that freedom was something you couldn't get enough of. This intrigued me.

Ali worked for a well-known supermarket chain, stacking shelves, though he had a degree. It was boring work; to get anywhere you had to grovel, or go to the bar and drink and exchange unpleasant banter. Sometimes you had to shake hands with women. Anyhow, the Asians didn't get promoted. A reason for this, he liked to muse, was that the major businesses were run by Jews. He applied for jobs all the time, but never got them. I couldn't see why this was so. He was certainly courteous. He brought me presents: a tie, mangos, the Koran. He was intellectually curious too, and liked showing me the new books he bought constantly. He knew a great deal about the history and politics of the Middle East, about which, he claimed, the average Westerner knew little. Ali knew the West, but the West didn't know him except through tendentious media images. The West, therefore, had no idea of its own arrogance, and was certainly not concerned about the extent to which it had no interest in anything outside itself.

Just when I thought there wasn't much Ali and I could argue about, he would say he didn't disapprove of the killings of journalists – and others – in Algeria. They were 'enemies'; he took it for granted that they were guilty. Perhaps, for him, the fact they were murdered made them guilty. During such conversations he liked to quote Malcolm X's phrase at me: 'By any means necessary', a modern motto of liberation thus becoming a tool of tyranny. I couldn't recall the context in which Malcolm X's phrase was first used, but it was clear that it could be applied to anything; its meaning had become unstable. These days not even language would hold still. Indeed, Ali himself could be called a 'fundamentalist' a word newly minted to mean a fanatical Muslim. It was a word he even applied to himself. At the same time he complained about Muslims being portrayed in the press as 'terrorists' and 'fanatics'. This argument, which had begun because of a book, continued to be about language and about what words mean, as much as anything.

The 'West' was a word, like liberalism, for anything bad. The West's freedom made him feel unsafe. If there was too much freedom you had to make less of it. I asked him about the difficulty of giving up things. He had been keen on clubs; he'd had an affair with a married woman. Renunciation made him feel strong, he said, while giving in made him feel weak. Wasn't the West full of addicts?

The West, therefore, was a place full of things he disliked – or where he liked to put them; and where people gave in to things he disapproved of. He gave me a flyer for a Muslim rally in Trafalgar Square that stated, 'Endemic crime, homosexuality, poverty, family breakdown, drug and alcohol abuse shows Western freedom and democracy just aren't working.' Because of this, Ali and his friends would never bring up their children here. But it also meant that he hated his own background, the forces that influenced him and the place he lived in.

His attitude kept reminding me of something I had heard before. Finally I realized it took me back to a paragraph in Czeslaw Milosz's *The Captive Mind* [Milosz is here referring to Eastern European communist intellectuals]: 'The official order is to evince the greatest horror of the West. Everything is evil there: trains are late, stores are empty, no one has money, people are poorly dressed, the highly praised technology is worthless. If you hear the name of a Western writer, painter or composer, you must scoff sarcastically, for to fight against "cosmopolitanism" is one of the basic duties of a citizen.'

Constraint could be a bulwark against a self that was always in danger of dissolving in the face of too much choice, opportunity and desire. By opposing that which continually changes around us, by denying those things we might want, we keep ourselves together. In the face of such decadent possibilities and corrupt pleasures – or where there is the fear of what free, or disobedient people might do – Islam would provide the necessary deprivation and could attenuate the repertoire of possible selves.

Open the Koran on almost any page and there is a threat. 'We have adorned the lowest heaven with lamps, missiles for pelting devils. We have prepared a scourge of flames for these, and the scourge of Hell for unbelievers: an evil fate!'

There is, then, sufficient regulation and punishment available. Without harsh constraint things might get out of hand, particularly in the post-modern world, where no one knows anything for sure. And so, against the 'corruption' of the West to which so many had innocently travelled, a new authority could be posited – that of Islam and, in particular, those who spoke for it. Without the revolutionary or opposing idea of Purity there wouldn't be those who knew what it was and could tell us when it had been violated. These men – and they were always men – became very powerful. The young invested a lot of authority in them.

Edward Said wrote: 'There are now immigrant communities in Europe from the former colonial territories to whom the ideas of "France" and "Britain" and "Germany" as constituted during the period between 1800 and 1950 simply excludes them.'

It must not be forgotten, therefore, that the backgrounds to the lives of these young people includes colonialism – being made to feel inferior in your own country. And then, in Britain, racism;

again, being made to feel inferior in your own country. My father's generation came to Britain full of hope and expectation. It would be an adventure, it would be difficult, but it would be worth it.

However, the settling in, with all the compromises and losses that that implies, has been more complicated and taken longer than anyone could imagine. Yet all along it was taken for granted that 'belonging', which means, in a sense, not having to notice where you are, and, more importantly, not being seen as different, would happen eventually. Where it hasn't, there is, in the children and grandchildren of the great post-war wave of immigrants, considerable anger and disillusionment. With some exceptions, Asians are still at the bottom of the pile; more likely to suffer from unemployment, poor housing, discrimination and ill-health. In a sense it hasn't worked out. The 'West' was a dream that didn't come true. But one cannot go home again. One is stuck.

Clearly this affects people in different ways. But without a doubt it is constraining, limiting, degrading, to be a victim in your own country. If you feel excluded it might be tempting to exclude others. The fundamentalists liked to reject the usual liberal pieties, sometimes for histrionic reasons. But their enemies – gays, Jews, the media, unsubmissive women, writers – were important to them. Their idea of themselves was based, like the M.C.C., or like any provincial snob, on who they excluded. Not only that, the central tenets of the West – democracy, pluralism, tolerance, which many people in Islamic countries, Muslim and non-Muslim alike, are struggling for – could be treated as a joke. For those whose lives had been negated by colonialism and racism such notions could only seem a luxury and of no benefit to them; they were a kind of hypocrisy.

Therefore, during our conversations Ali continuously argued that there are no such things as freedom or democracy, or that those abstractions were only real for a small group. For him, if they didn't exist in the purest possible form, they didn't exist at all. Milosz might call Ali's attitude, with some sadness, 'disappointed love', and it was a disappointment that seemed to attach itself to everything. Which isn't to say there wasn't hope too. For instance, he believed that when the existing corrupt rulers of Muslim countries were swept away, they would be replaced by 'true' Muslims, benign in every way, who would work for the benefit of the people, according to the word of God. If the present was unsatisfactory and impossible to live in, as it always would be for him, there was the perfect future, which would, probably, safely remain the future – the best place for it, for his purposes.

Fundamentalism provides security. For the fundamentalist, as for all reactionaries, everything has been decided. Truth has been agreed and nothing must change. For serene liberals on the other hand, the consolations of knowing seem less satisfying than the pleasures of puzzlement, and of wanting to discover for oneself. But the feeling that one cannot know everything, that there will always be maddening and live questions about who one is and how it is possible to make a life with other people who don't accept one, can be devastating. Perhaps it is only for so long that one can live with that kind of puzzlement. Rationalists have always underestimated the need people have for belief. Enlightenment values – rationalism, tolerance, scepticism – don't get you through a dreadful night; they don't provide spiritual comfort or community or solidarity. Fundamentalist Islam could do this in a country that was supposed to be home but which could, from day to day, seem alien.

Muslim fundamentalism has always seemed to me to be profoundly wrong, unnecessarily restrictive and frequently cruel. But there are reasons for its revival that are comprehensible. It is this that has made me want to look at it not only in terms of ideas, but in stories, in character, in terms of what people do. For a writer there cannot be just one story, a story to end all stories in which everything is said, but as many stories as one wants, serving all sorts of purposes and sometimes none at all. The primary object, though, is to provide pleasure of different kinds. And one must remember that perhaps the greatest book of all, and certainly one of the most pleasurable, *The One Thousand and One Nights* is, like the Koran, written in Arabic. This creativity, the making of something that didn't exist before, the vigour and stretch of a living imagination, is a human affirmation of another kind, and a necessary and important form of self-examination. Without it our humanity is diminished.

Hanif Kureishi, 1997

My Son the Fanatic

EXT. FINGERHUT HOUSE – DAY

A large modern house in the country, surrounded by land.

INT. LIVING ROOM. FINGERHUT HOUSE – DAY

In the living room. Mrs Fingerhut, prim, snobbish, middle-class, has been entertaining the assembled group for some time, as Fingerhut is late.

The atmosphere is strained. Mrs Fingerhut's daughter Madelaine, Parvez, Minoo and their son Farid – all in their best clothes – sit on hard chairs. Parvez is both terrified and ecstatic to be there.

Mrs Fingerhut puts down a photograph album she has been showing everyone.

> MRS FINGERHUT
> Madelaine was a delightful girl.
> > (*pause*)
> She still is, of course.

Madelaine and Farid, both uncomfortable, glance at one another.

> PARVEZ
> > (*smiling at her*)
> And a little bit plumpish at times . . . as you said, twice.

> MINOO
> Rice is very good.

Mrs Fingerhut looks bewildered.

> For reducing diet.

> PARVEZ
> Cricket is excellent. Farid was Captain. I warned, don't you ever go professional, career is over in five years. Mrs Fingerhut – Hilda – this boy of ours, I can assure you he is

3

all-round-type; going whole hog, but not on field!

MINOO

Oh yes. But in garden?

PARVEZ
(*to Minoo, sharply*)

One minute.
(*to Mrs Fingerhut*)
At school he carried the prizes home. Now at college he is . . .
he is top student of year.

MADELAINE

Not difficult.

Mrs Fingerhut looks at Madelaine, who scratches. Farid smirks. They sit there a moment: tense.

EXT. FINGERHUT HOUSE – DAY

Fingerhut's chauffeur-driven car turns into the drive, stopping beside Parvez's battered taxi, which Fingerhut regards with aversion as he walks past it. The house dogs rush towards him, barking.

INT. LIVING ROOM. FINGERHUT HOUSE – DAY

PARVEZ
(*hushed voice*)

The Chief Inspector.

MRS FINGERHUT
(*going to the door*)

About time.

PARVEZ

The law never sleeps at night.

Looks at Farid, who is cringing.

Perhaps a career in the police could be guaranteed for you.
Let me mention it to Chief Inspector.

FARID

Papa.

5

PARVEZ

Leave the matters of business opening to me. Put on cheerful face – blast it! – this is happiest occasion of life.

MINOO
(*in Urdu, subtitled*)
I want the toilet.

PARVEZ
(*in Urdu, subtitled*)
Not again. They'll think we're Bengalis.

MINOO
They couldn't tell the difference between a Pakistani and a Bengali. We're all –

Minoo is halted by the expression on Parvez's face.

Fingerhut grandly enters the room and looks around at everyone. Parvez goes to him, kissingly.

CUT TO:

Fingerhut and Parvez together. Farid watches this, embarrassed and repelled.

PARVEZ

I will arrange all engagement party details personally. Our tradition is beautiful in this respect.

Fingerhut appears to make a face.

You enjoy our food when I bring it personally to police station.
(*leaning closer*)
Chief Inspector, please inform me absolutely in confidence: Farid is top police material, isn't he?

FINGERHUT
Isn't he training to be an accountant?

PARVEZ
Law and order might be more reliable. Crime is everywhere out of control, wouldn't you confirm?

6

Looking at Farid, who is cringing.

My boy says the same.

                    FINGERHUT
He would know, would he?

CUT TO:

                    PARVEZ
                 (*to Minoo*)
Get camera. Now is moment!

CUT TO:

                 (*to Fingerhut*)
Please, sir, would a pose be all right for private use
exclusively?

Fingerhut appears to nod.

                 (*to Minoo*)
Bring champagne, too.

Minoo pulls a camera and a bottle of champagne out of a bag.

CUT TO:

*A photograph is being taken, by the chauffeur, of the whole group. Mrs
Fingerhut stands next to Parvez, who has his arm around Farid.
Madelaine is beside Farid. Minoo and Chief Inspector Fingerhut.*

*We see all the faces. There is a flash. Other photographs, in other
combinations. And finally, Parvez and Farid together – both drinking
champagne, clinking glasses, Parvez laughing to himself.*

Titles in.

INT. CAR – NIGHT

*We cut inside the car and pull back from one of the photographs – now
a little curled and yellowing. Then, Parvez's face, as he gesticulates,
shakes his head and waves at other drivers; we see him singing to
himself.*

7

Low on the track, an Asian radio station is playing Nusrat Fateh Ali Khan, or something similar.

Parvez is a Pakistani in his early fifties. He wears an old suit, scuffed shoes and inevitably looks scruffy. He is unshaven in places, his hair stands up, his askew tie is stained, his sweater unravelling. But he is a lively and engaging man with a lovely face.

EXT. NORTHERN CITY – NIGHT

A high shot – a Northern city.

EXT. STREET

Parvez's taxi cab drives through the frame – away from the city.

EXT. AIRPORT – NIGHT

We see the flickering lights, planes overhead, open air, foreign travel – and Businessmen with briefcases hurrying through the exits.

INT. AIRPORT – NIGHT

Parvez stands by the barrier with a cardboard sign that says 'SHIT' in large letters. A smaller letter, 's' has been added to the end of this legend.

Parvez keeps getting elbowed aside by the other taxi-drivers, but he is tenacious; he pushes forward and waves the sign at a likely figure, who backs away when he sees the piece of cardboard.

Behind this man the German strides through the gate.

INT./EXT. CAR

   CUT TO:

Parvez's talking mouth.

He is driving the man into town.

PARVEZ
You are brand-new in town, sir?

GERMAN

That's why I passed through the airport a few minutes ago.

PARVEZ

Ah-uh. Interested to see something of our glory, sir?

This is an opportunity for Parvez to show off his knowledge of his adopted city, its geography and history. He talks about the mills, the great nineteenth-century entrepreneurs, the first Pakistani immigrants, and he points out their shops. (He begins cautiously, to see whether the passenger will respond, and then becomes more voluble.) It is an animated if garbled flow, and we should have shots of the relevant places.

The German is amused and interested by Parvez, who, encouraged, continues, until . . .

INT./EXT. RESTAURANT – NIGHT

They pass the large and swanky front of an Indian restaurant where Parvez slows down and stops.

PARVEZ

Good, good, final decoration is done. Here we will be having my son's getting engaged party. He is marrying Madelaine, Madelaine Fingerhut, the top policeman's daughter. He impressed her no end. I am working extensive hours to make the money.

He turns round.

The restaurant, sir, belongs to my friend, Fizzy. There, fattish one. We came together to this country. He had five pounds, which he borrowed from me. Look now. And look at me!

We see Fizzy, avuncular and affluent in a good but loud suit, greeting guests at the door. Parvez beeps his horn and waves.

Your name too small on front, yaar!

Fizzy notices Parvez with some irritation. The place he has recently opened is trying to be posh. He comes over.

FIZZY
Don't block parking space! Come – eat!

PARVEZ
I'm eating to capacity, when I get one minute of silence!

FIZZY
I must have date of engagement party.

PARVEZ
Yes, yes, coming up.

FIZZY
(*sharply*)
Tomorrow for definite.

Parvez is surprised by this tone, and indicates the passenger in the back.

PARVEZ
Okay, okay.

Fizzy gives Parvez his card and winks. Parvez hands it to the German.

(*driving on*)
Top class place, almost. You like our food?

I try everything.

Parvez considers this, before turning the car in another direction.

INT./EXT. SEEDY STREETS – NIGHT

CUT TO:

The cab now passes a row of unprepossessing Prostitutes in a seedy nineteenth-century street. Several of the women are perilously young and the others, in their mid-thirties, some black, and one in her mid-forties carrying a little dog, are standing in the wind and cold, stamping their feet, awaiting trade.

The German perks up and turns around in his seat.

PARVEZ

Local people and religious types don't like. Condom and all, you know, hanging from rose-bushes.

EXT. SMART HOTEL – NIGHT

The city's smartest hotel. Parvez staggers with a bag in each hand and one under each arm to the door of the hotel, where he knows the Porters. He isn't fit and his back hurts. He stops and rubs his lower spine, before proceeding painfully.

The German gives him a good tip. Parvez shakes his hand and gives him his card.

PARVEZ
(*after attempting some German*)

Thank you, sir. And please, sir, let's meet again. Call me personally by name, Parvez. That's me. Or at home.

INT. CAR – NIGHT

Parvez sitting in his car. With the tip on one side, he counts the day's takings. Then he counts it again, unable to believe it is so little.

The voice of the Controller on the radio interrupts him. Parvez tries to compose himself.

INT. NIGHTCLUB – NIGHT

The early hours of the morning. Parvez standing in the entrance to a nightclub, chatting with the white Bouncers, who are condescending.

Through a spangled curtain we see coloured lights and hear music. (We see this club later.)

PARVEZ

The Chief Inspector – all Fingerhuts are close personal friends of mine – is very concerned about scene of nightclubs, noises and all. But I've told him –

BOUNCER
(*after glancing inside*)

Your ride.

A white man crashes through the curtain, and Bettina follows him.

INT./EXT. STREET OUTSIDE CLUB. AND IN CAR

Parvez follows them to the car. The Man is high-spirited but almost collapses on the back seat.

MAN

Turn it up!

PARVEZ
(*turns on a Tony Bennett record*)
Romantic tune for romantic evening, sir?

INT./EXT. STREET AND IN CAR

The white Man is groping and fondling Bettina – who both placates him and keeps him away. Parvez watches them in his mirror.

MAN
(*to Parvez*)
Stop, stop! I'm going in my pants!

PARVEZ

Do not water new upholstery, sir!

Parvez halts hastily, rushes round to the backseat and hauls the Man out of the car.

CUT TO:

The Man is pissing against the wall outside a row of Asian shops.

PARVEZ

I told a German about you. Rich-smelling. New in town.

BETTINA
(*surprised*)

Ta very much. You'll be wanting commission next.

PARVEZ

Am I later taking you home?

BETTINA
(*indicating punter*)

He's paid for an all-night job, but I think he's looking a bit on the bright side.

PARVEZ

I will wait, then.

BETTINA

Will you? Thanks. How have you been?

PARVEZ

Same. You know, I liked –

BETTINA

What?

PARVEZ

Our little talk –

BETTINA

Several talks –

The Man staggers against the side of the car, and falls in again.

PARVEZ

Please sir, no smoking indoors, smell is deafening.

The Man grabs Parvez by the back of the neck.

MAN

Go!

Parvez reaches down for the thick piece of wood he uses to defend himself.

> PARVEZ
>
> Don't touch me, sir, in case I go left instead of right.

The Man drags the rear-view mirror to one side and adopts an Indian accent and waggles his head.

> MAN
>
> Look straight ahead, sir!

INT. CAR

As they drive, the Man fucks Bettina in the back of the car. As Parvez hears the Man cry out, we cut to:

INT. BEDROOM OF TERRACED HOUSE – NIGHT

The noise of a clattering dustbin lid awakens a middle-aged Pakistani woman asleep in bed.

INT./EXT. WINDOW OF TERRACED HOUSE – NIGHT

The Pakistani woman hurries to the window and is alarmed to see the shadowy figure of a man rooting in the bins.

EXT. BACK OF TERRACED HOUSE – NIGHT

Parvez is examining the contents of his own dustbins. Along with the remains of many messy Indian dinners, he pulls out LPs and CDs, as well as crumpled posters of rock and sporting heroes.

EXT. BACK OF HOUSE – NIGHT

The back door of the house opens. A light is switched on, illuminating him. Parvez's wife Minoo – in her nightie and dressing-gown – looks nervously around the door.

Parvez looks up, ignores her, and then holds something up to the light and examines it.

> MINOO
>
> Papu, it is you? I was frightened.

He grunts.

You are like a dirty tramp.

PARVEZ
Why does he throw this rubbish out?

MINOO
He has always been a clean boy.

Parvez comes towards her. She can see him now. He moves quickly past her.

PARVEZ
(*bitterly*)
Why can you never give a straight answer!

INT. FARID'S BEDROOM – NIGHT

Quietly Parvez opens the door to his son's bedroom. He is about to venture a few tiptoed paces into the room when Minoo, behind him, pulls him out and shuts the door.

INT. UPSTAIRS LANDING – NIGHT

Minoo watches Parvez to ensure he doesn't go back in.

PARVEZ
Don't stand there like the police!

INT. FIZZY'S RESTAURANT – EVENING

The restaurant is almost full with well-off whites, and a few besuited and bejewelled Asians. Fizzy is unctuously elaborating over a white couple – opening napkins, pouring wine, discussing the menu.

Parvez looks a bit out of place in his crumpled clothes, but he surveys everything keenly: the fountains, the fancy foliage, the comfy sofas and Indian effects. A Waiter hurries towards him.

WAITER
He say wait in function suite. Busy in here.

INT. FUNCTION ROOM IN FIZZY'S RESTAURANT – EVENING

Kept waiting, Parvez has been walking about disconsolately in a large room above the restaurant, which is full of broken chairs, boxes, and unwanted kitchen equipment.

FIZZY
(*coming in hurriedly*)
I'm rushing, but here we can have food on tables. Another small kitchen there. I'll make it magnificent for entire Fingerhut tribe! and there –

PARVEZ
And the food not too . . . fierce, yaar?

FIZZY
What?

PARVEZ
Toilet is far away for older guests.

Fizzy isn't much amused by this.

FIZZY
But why is date not fixed? What problem is going on?

PARVEZ
No, no, I am awaiting full confirmation from high up.

FIZZY
Your boy is taking you up in the world – at last.
(*beat*)
One time a fare said to me, 'So what's new in the taxi business?' I racked my head and . . . there was nothing but abuses and little money. That was the day I threw down my keys, cleared out and took a loan. Do or die, yaar.

PARVEZ
Some of us have become traffic wardens but personally you'll never find me walking alone. All I want is to pay mortgage.

FIZZY
Maybe you will – five minutes before you die, eh?

Parvez turns and walks away.

16

That will please Minoo at last, eh?

PARVEZ

Oh God.

FIZZY

She is very strong-willed, yaar. You never got her under control, that has been problem.

They look at one another. As they walk away they slap one another on the back, consolingly; old friends.

EXT. STREET OUTSIDE CAB OFFICE – NIGHT

Later that night.

This is a seedy part of town. Two Prostitutes can be seen touting for custom across the street as Parvez pulls up in his cab outside the office. He looks across the street at the Prostitutes, but Bettina isn't amongst them.

Other cabs and their loquacious Drivers, leaning against the bonnets of their cars, smoking and gossiping, are lined up outside the office.

INT. CAB OFFICE – NIGHT

Parvez enters to find a Prostitute waiting. Rashid, another driver, younger than Parvez and rather aggressive, has been joshing her.

PROSTITUTE

Parvez, take me back home, my kids are on their own. I'm not going with any of these –

RASHID

It's useless going with Parvez – he accepts only money!

PROSTITUTE

Fuck off, Rashid, I'll pay you tomorrow!

PARVEZ
(*in a hurry*)

Not now.

PROSTITUTE

Don't be a bastard! Sorry, sorry, I didn't mean it!

17

Parvez moves away from her towards a door leading to an inner office which is occupied by the Radio Controller, visible through a glass panel in the walls.

Rashid puts his arm around the Prostitute's shoulders and laughs.

RASHID

Pay me later – and if you can't –

Rashid puts his hand up her skirt and pinches her, much to the raucous amusement of the others.

INT. RADIO ROOM OF CAB OFFICE – NIGHT

Parvez enters the room to find the Controller very busy talking to cabs on the road, taking bookings etc.

This is a larger area of busted furniture. A TV with a video showing Indian action films. A boys' school atmosphere: men playing cards, stuffing their faces with chapatis, talking, shouting out jokes.

Two Men are arm-wrestling over a table, with others watching, urging them on. This wrestling contest continues throughout the film – with sometimes one man about to win, and sometimes the other. There is never a result.

The Controller is pleased to see Parvez, but this conversation is interrupted by calls.

CONTROLLER

Parvez, yaar, I never speak to you in flesh! How's the exam boy? He studies more than anyone in country.

PARVEZ

These sons can be a bag of trouble, yaar.

CONTROLLER

Everyone know Javad's boy got in jail. They say it Javad's fault. How's the engagement coming? Everyone say you don't get parking tickets now.

PARVEZ

Tell the truth, Farid has gone very far inside himself these days –

CONTROLLER
Up and down, yaar, rather than in and out?

*Just as the Controller sees his friend is troubled, Parvez cuts the
conversation short. Through the glass pane he has seen Bettina enter the
outer office.*

PARVEZ
(*to the Controller*)
Thanks for the extra work.

CONTROLLER
You're looking tired, yaar.
(*shouts after him and around at the other drivers*)

But no one slacking!

The Controller watches Parvez and Bettina go.

EXT. CAB OFFICE – NIGHT

Bettina and Parvez come out of the office and get into Parvez's cab.

BETTINA
Have you eaten today?

PARVEZ
Which day is it?

BETTINA
Come on

Parvez drives off.

EXT. MOBILE ROADSIDE CAFE – EARLY MORNING

*A lay-by on a windy hillside overlooking the city. A mobile cafe/catering
van. Bacon sizzling on a hot-plate. The Owner, whom Parvez and
Bettina both know, squirts mustard into the bacon butties, looks at
Parvez, and squirts more in. They laugh.*

*Parvez bites into his sandwich with pleasure, sighs, and considers the
night and the landscape. Bettina stands beside him, enjoying her butty,
licking her fingers, ogled by a couple of lorry drivers parked nearby.*

PARVEZ

For weeks I haven't slept ten minutes. He throws away his
things. He won't talk. Who would have sons?

BETTINA

Will you say something about what you've noticed?

PARVEZ

I am observing daily. I don't want to be some fool interfering
with his freedoms. He gets easily rude with me now – his
mother's side of the family.

BETTINA

What does your wife say?

Parvez is about to reply, but just shakes his head.

INT./EXT. TAXI – EARLY MORNING

*Bettina takes a tape from her bag, puts it in the cassette-player and
fiddles with it until she finds the piece of music she wants to hear.
(Maybe a reggae track.) She listens then, leaning her head back, hums
and smokes. Parvez glances at her. He is about to tell her something –
but her good mood and company relaxes him.*

BETTINA

I haven't seen you for a few days.

PARVEZ

I'm going further and further afield for work, but earning
less. They're sacking the drivers who won't work night
and day. Sometimes I think – if I hit that tree what
difference?

BETTINA

You wouldn't see that.

INT./EXT. TAXI – EARLY MORNING

*As the taxi reaches the top of a hill they are confronted with a view
of the dales. But they are looking at one another – with some
curiosity.*

BETTINA

Can we walk?

PARVEZ

Walk?

BETTINA

In the fresh air. The breeze is lovely. Let me show you a place.

PARVEZ

Surely there is air everywhere about?

She laughs and gets out of the car. He has no choice but to follow her.

EXT. THE DALES – EARLY MORNING

Bettina and Parvez walking away from the car. Bettina enjoys herself, but Parvez is uncertain. Suddenly she runs down a hill. Parvez has no choice but to follow, unathletically.

CUT TO:

She approaches a stream. On a far side is a ruin on a hill, surrounded by trees. This is the spot Bettina wanted to show him and, although he is breathless and finding it hard going, its beauty impresses him.

BETTINA

Well?

PARVEZ

Yes, it is magnificent. There were places, back home, I used to go.

(*he laughs*)

With a girl, actually.

Bettina looks at him, before skipping across the stream. Parvez follows uncertainly. Halfway across, his foot slips on the wet stones and he finds himself standing knee-deep in water.

PARVEZ

Oh God, there are icicles going inside!

BETTINA

Those trousers will have to come off.

He looks at her in horror and she laughs.

INT. PARVEZ'S HOUSE – EARLY MORNING

We see Minoo trying to scrub Parvez's shoes in the kitchen, his trousers are hanging up to dry.

PARVEZ'S LIVING ROOM

Parvez is in the living room. He's changed into salwar kurta, and is sipping a glass of whisky and relishing the taste, in a good mood. Minoo comes into the room.

MINOO

We can't afford new shoes. You're not a coolie to carry baggage through mud.

PARVEZ

There are many abnormal occurrences in taxi business.

MINOO

Not usually involving a wet bottom.

PARVEZ

Hamid had to transport a tortoise in a box to Newcastle.

(*pause*)

There was a strange building last night, which reminded me of your grandfather's house in Multan. All tumbled down, like his after the hurricane.

MINOO

Take me, Papu.

He puts his bare feet into her lap. She caresses them.

PARVEZ

I must speak with Farid.

MINOO

About what?

PARVEZ
(*thinks*)

Engagement party.

She works on his feet.

Minny, how has Fizzy done so well?

MINOO

He was always greedy . . . for things.

PARVEZ

He was a greedy little boy.

MINOO

You are easily made happy and like things to be always the same. That's why you never made a success.

PARVEZ

Not a success?

MINOO

Driving taxi for twenty-five years is not –

PARVEZ

All right.

MINOO

If I'd been given your freedom . . . think what I would have done . . .

BETTINA

What such marvellous stuff then, bloody hell?

MINOO

I would have studied. I would have gone everywhere. And talked . . . talked.

PARVEZ

Talked – who the hell to?

MINOO

Anyone. And not stood here day after day washing filthy trousers.

PARVEZ

It's easy to say.

She gets up and goes.

CUT TO:

Parvez is contemplating a display of Farid's cricket and swimming trophies on the mantelpiece. Also, a photograph of him, with a cricket team, holding a cup.

INT. LIVING ROOM. PARVEZ'S HOUSE – MORNING

Minoo is hoovering the muddy footprints from the carpet around the bottom of Parvez's trousers. Parvez has fallen asleep on the sofa. Some of Farid's discarded belongings lie alongside the empty bottle on the floor.

The front door slams. Parvez wakes up.

INT. LIVING ROOM WINDOW OF PARVEZ'S HOUSE – MORNING

He goes to the window and sees Farid in the street arguing with Madelaine, who has just turned up.

Also parked outside, with its boot open, is a car belonging to a young Asian man. Farid has handed him a guitar, amp and speaker.

This conversation is from Parvez's POV through the window. He can't make out much of it.

MADELAINE

I only wanted to see you –

FARID
(*coldly*)
I told you truth from day one, and everything has been discussed several times –

MADELAINE

Oh, what has happened to you –

FARID

Leave me in peace –

She turns to go.

Don't come again!

We see Farid watching her go. At one point she turns. The two of them look at one another.

EXT. PARVEZ'S HOUSE – DAY

Parvez standing at the window.

EXT. PARVEZ'S HOUSE – DAY

Parvez runs barefoot out of his house to confront Farid.

PARVEZ

Where is she going?

Farid shrugs.

Why are you fighting?

FARID

Why do people fight?

PARVEZ

What is problem here? Farid, can I help you?

FARID

Papa –

Farid's Asian Companion is getting impatient.

Farid –

Farid puts the rest of the stuff in the car and the Companion gives him a wad of money which he immediately pockets.

PARVEZ
(*to Farid*)
Where is that going? You used to love making a terrible noise with these instruments!

Farid bends his knees and imitates a ridiculous rock guitarist.

FARID
You said all the time that there are more important things than 'Stairway to Heaven'. You couldn't have been more right, Papa.

PARVEZ
Y-Y-Yes.
(*pause*)
Where are you going?

Farid looks down at Parvez's bare feet.

FARID
To college. Go inside, you'll catch pneumonia.

Farid picks Parvez up in his arms and carries him indoors – Parvez continues to talk all the while.

PARVEZ
I've been driving twelve, fourteen hours non-stop. Many times I've gone through the red light. Everywhere I am hurting. It is hell on wheels.

FARID
Don't do it for me.

PARVEZ
Who else to do it for?

Farid puts him down and then turns and continues up the street.

Farid . . .?

Parvez turns back. Minoo has gone. His clean shoes stand in the middle of the hall.

INT. FARID'S BEDROOM – DAY

Parvez surveys Farid's almost bare room. Even last night's boxes have gone, and the shelves are practically bare. On the walls are the marks of removed posters and pictures.

He sees, sticking out from under the bed, the handle of a cricket bat. He pulls it out. On it are the signatures of a triumphant Pakistani cricket team captained by Imran Khan.

CUT TO:

In a drawer he finds an airline ticket – which he examines.

CUT TO:

As he goes, Parvez picks up a discarded folder full of photographs of Farid, which he has had professionally taken to get modelling work.

Next to it is a piece of crumpled-up paper which Parvez tosses in the air and hits across the room at the door, just as Minoo comes in, surprising him.

                    MINOO
You know how you complain when your food goes cold.

As he follows her to the door he picks up the crumpled piece of paper. It is a signed picture of Madelaine and Farid – taken during the opening scene – with lipstick kisses on it and the words: 'Love you always, handsome'.

INT. HOUSE – DAY

He goes downstairs, examining the picture, and is about to speak to Minoo, but sees she is on the phone, at the bottom of the stairs.

                    MINOO
There is someone calling you. A . . . shit.

                    PARVEZ
Shh . . . Minoo!

(*He takes the receiver. Realizes who it is.*)
Ah, Herr, Mr Schitz, coming, coming, directly on call,
immediate service.

EXT. DISUSED VICTORIAN MILL COMPLEX – DAY

*Parvez drives up to the mill gates with the German – Schitz – where a
group of suited Asian and white Businessmen are waiting, holding
briefcases.*

GERMAN
(*as he gets out*)
One hour.

*Parvez watches the German being received deferentially by the
Businessmen.*

*Parvez drives off fast – the crumpled photograph of Madelaine and
Farid on the dashboard in front of him.*

INT. BANK – DAY

A big imposing place.

*Parvez walks quickly through the – mostly white – queue, embarrassed
but determined, and in a hurry.*

PARVEZ
Sorry, sorry. Urgent personal matter.

*He stops and stares at the official he's seeking – Madelaine. She's
pretty, but thin and fragile-looking.*

PARVEZ
Is that Madelaine? Miss Fingerhut.

She looks up at him and nods.

Farid's dad – Parvez and all.

MADELAINE
(*to customer*)
Excuse me.

Now Parvez is there he doesn't quite know what to say.

PARVEZ

Food is waiting anytime. Why not come Sunday, eh?

MADELAINE

We've packed up.

PARVEZ

Engagement is off?

MADELAINE

He didn't tell you?

PARVEZ

Suddenly you don't like my boy?

MADELAINE

He wanted to start again, with new friends.

PARVEZ

What type of friends?

MADELAINE

I wanted to meet them. Didn't want to be narrow like some folks round here. But they wouldn't –

PARVEZ

What?

MADELAINE

Meet women.

PARVEZ

Everyone wants to meet women, surely!

MADELAINE

I thought you were arranging a marriage for him? A month ago he took me out to tell me.

PARVEZ

But all this time I have been preparing party!

MADELAINE

He wanted someone he had more in common with. He has become inflexible.

She shakes her head. Behind Parvez people are complaining.

I have been ill.

PARVEZ

I will break open his face until he obeys!
(*thinks*)
Best thing – I will discuss with your father.

MADELAINE

You don't know anything, do you?

Parvez looks at her. Madelaine is reluctant to repeat the slur.

Farid told my father he was the only pig he'd ever wanted to eat.

Parvez looks at her in horror.

EXT. WEAVING SHED – DAY

Parvez drives fast up to the gates only to find the area deserted. Annoyed by missing his appointment he gets out of the cab and runs around the deserted buildings in the hope of finding the German. The mill is vast and his footsteps echo around the massive silent buildings.

Parvez notices a door has been left unlocked. He enters.

INT. WEAVING SHED – DAY

Parvez peers around the dark cavern of the shed, empty except for a few odd bits of broken machinery.

As he is about to go outside again the German's voice rings out. He is standing outside a cabin on a platform some twenty feet off the floor.

GERMAN

We should have a party here.

Parvez looks around, confused, for the source of the voice, and makes his way towards the German until he is standing at the foot of the ladder leading to the cabin.

PARVEZ

Mr Schitz, here I had my first job in England. Fizzy and I. Five years double shift, seven day a week. They wouldn't put me in the team.

GERMAN
(*laughs*)
I wouldn't put you in the management team either.

PARVEZ
Cricket team. We were the best players. I could spin a little.

He trots across the floor and illustrates how he could bowl. The German laughs.

What business are you doing here?

GERMAN
Out of town shopping. Everything under one roof.

PARVEZ
The land and the labour is cheap, eh?

GERMAN
Like the women. Remind me – what is the name of the one you recommended?

PARVEZ
Bettina.

GERMAN

Tried her yourself?

PARVEZ

Sir, I only joke with them and all.

GERMAN

I want to see her. Where do you boys hang out?

PARVEZ

Not nice place, sir –

GERMAN

Let's go, little man. Instruct her to be there. And tell her to wear boots.
(*sings*)
Spanish boots of Spanish leather.

EXT. ROUGH PUB – DAY

Parvez follows the striding German up to the pub. Several taxis are parked outside.

INT. ROUGH PUB

This is a rough and noisy place frequented by Prostitutes, Taxi-Drivers, Local Lads, Drug Dealers.

As Parvez crosses the pub a fellow Driver addresses him.

DRIVER

Getting sociable at last, Parvez, eh?

PARVEZ

Working as usual, yaar.

GERMAN

These are all your colleagues?

PARVEZ

Sir, a lot of these drivers are very low-class types. They can hardly speak English.

GERMAN

You're not a snob are you, Parvez?

PARVEZ

The 'gentleman' is my code.

GERMAN

And it stops you enjoying women?

PARVEZ

There is respect, sir, but not degradation.

GERMAN

Respect is no substitute for pleasure. What of life do you
enjoy then?

Parvez looks puzzled.

Your family?

Parvez nods unconvincingly.

I left mine.

PARVEZ

That's not a very nice thing, sir.

GERMAN

What do you know about it?

CUT TO:

Bettina walks in.

PARVEZ

There, sir.

The German looks at her approvingly.

GERMAN
(*to Parvez*)

We boys are going to start to enjoy ourselves.

She comes over and stands by the table.

PARVEZ

Bettina.

*The German gets up kisses her hand. The other Prostitutes and Drivers
watch with some interest.*

GERMAN

Couldn't you just kiss every part of her?

BETTINA
(*to Parvez of the German, with considerable charm*)
Couldn't you just kick every part of *him*?

Parvez looks nervous. The German laughs, then turns to the barman and gives him a twenty-pound note.

GERMAN

Get her a drink!
(*to Bettina*)
Have some lunch.
(*to Parvez*)
Good. Very good. Let's go.

He heads for the door. Bewildered, Parvez follows, shrugging apologetically to Bettina. She snatches the twenty-pound note from the barman and pockets it.

EXT. TAXI OUTSIDE PROSTITUTE'S HOUSE/STREET – NIGHT

Parvez pulls up outside the house. Bettina gets in.

As they drive away they're startled by a drug-addict Prostitute jumping out and banging on the window.

PROSTITUTE

Bastard, bastard, giving her a lift! Bettina always gets her ride, does she? What about me!

Parvez accelerates. Bettina turns and watches the woman.

PARVEZ

She wanted a ride but didn't have no money.

BETTINA

All her money goes into her arm. She even sold her floorboards. You didn't buy any did you? They were riddled – like her.

PARVEZ
(*alarmed*)
Is that what drug types do?

34

She looks at him.

Parvez has parked the car with a view over the moors or hillside. Over the radio we hear the Car Controller calling for Parvez, who turns down the volume.

We see the concentrating faces of Parvez and Bettina, and her hand – its rings and bracelets – as she sketches a joint, various pills, a pile of coke, etc.

> BETTINA
> (*gently*)
> Look out for sweats, mood changes, frequent visits to the bog. Also, the eyes. Are they big or small, bloodshot, tired . . . vacant. And his arms –

Parvez is listening carefully and nodding. He looks down at Bettina's legs; her coat has come open, her underwear is exposed. He is stirred.

Bettina notices him looking at her. She passes the piece of paper to him. There is an intimate moment between them as they regard one another.

> PARVEZ
> It's better the other drivers don't know this. They are envious of Farid winning the prizes. But you have always seen what I am so concerned about.

> BETTINA
> You talk about Farid a lot. And you like to hear about my daughters. The other drivers like to pretend they don't have families.

> PARVEZ
> He used to love his clothes. At weekends he worked in those fashion shops. I've never known a boy with such enthusiasm for ironing. I was worried he'd gone homo. I told you, he did some modelling. In London they wanted him. I thought – anything he wants he can do. Now he has become – I never before cursed the day I brought us to this country.

EXT. PARVEZ'S HOUSE – DAY

Parvez arrives outside his house to see Farid putting a box full of his things into the boot of a friend's car before going back into the house. Parvez gets out of the cab and, giving the driver a perfunctory nod, goes in.

INT. PARVEZ'S HOUSE – DAY

As Parvez enters he sees serious Farid, carrying a cardboard box under his arm, coming downstairs and making for the front door.

PARVEZ

Why are you getting rid of those things? Farid!

CUT TO:

Parvez is consulting Bettina's piece of paper.

CUT TO:

Parvez follows Farid. When he catches up with him, he takes the box from him and puts it down. While holding him, Parvez looks into his eyes. Minoo comes out of another room.

PARVEZ

Put light on, Minoo.

She does so. Parvez gets closer. Then he takes Farid's hand and pushes up his sleeve. Farid gives in, leaning back against the wall and letting him do it, staring sardonically into his father's eyes.

Parvez glances mechanically at Farid's arm, not really knowing what to look for. Farid slowly rolls down his sleeve and does up the buttons.

FARID

I can always tell when you've been reading the *Daily Express*.

EXT. PARVEZ'S HOUSE

Farid goes out of the front door to a waiting car into which he puts the box before heading back to his room. Parvez gets his breath back and continues to follow him.

PARVEZ

Farid, please, do me the credit here, yaar, tell me something!
Why make me into the fool?

Minoo is packing the remaining discarded items into another box and generally helping to clear out the room.

As Farid passes him, Parvez tries another tone.

Madelaine not coming over tonight? Why not?
(*his blood pressure is rising*)
That's what I'm asking here.

Farid shakes his head as he walks past.

PARVEZ

Where are you going?

FARID

To see Asad.

MINOO

I'll get your coat.

PARVEZ

Playing squash?

Farid shakes his head.

Have you got rid of the racket I bought?

He and Farid look at one another. Pause.

I worked my arse to pay for that – overtime!

MINOO
(*standing at the door*)
All the time you shout and swear! That's why no one speaks
here! Let him go, you useless –!

PARVEZ

Useless? Who earns the money!

37

MINOO

I don't know what games you play out there in the mud, but it's practically nothing now –

PARVEZ

Who spends it!

MINOO

There's nothing to spend after all these years! Look at Fizzy. His wife went on a cruise.

PARVEZ

Ex-wife. All you do is send my money to your lazy relatives! What are they eating there – diamonds?

MINOO

I wish I were with them.

PARVEZ

Go then!

To Farid, desperate to retrieve the subject.

I met Madelaine.

Farid looks at Minoo. The mood changes.

Yes! What about the engagement, and this other marriage I am arranging, eh?

FARID

I am intending to marry.

Minoo nods approvingly.

PARVEZ

Yes, Madelaine is so nice. Minoo has written to all three people she knows in Lahore, announcing.

FARID

I have asked trusted people for a suitable girl.

PARVEZ

You go to them secretly when I have hand-picked Miss Fingerhut!

(*pause*)

You used to kiss her?

MINOO

Stop!

PARVEZ

Is it wrong to find out if our son is normal, eh?

MINOO

Normal is not perverted like in your mind.

PARVEZ

Keep quiet!

FARID
(*intervening*)

You might not have noticed – Madelaine is so different.

PARVEZ

How?

FARID

Can you put keema with strawberries?

Surprised by this, Parvez moves closer to his son who hesitatingly continues.

In the end our cultures . . . they cannot be mixed.

PARVEZ

Everything is mingling already together, this thing and the other!

FARID

Some of us are wanting something more besides muddle.

PARVEZ

What?

FARID

Belief, purity, belonging to the past.
(*beat*)
I won't bring up my children in this country.

What types are these new friends?

Minoo goes to Parvez. She is trying to get him out of the room.

MINOO
They are not like the bad English stealing and drugging.

PARVEZ
How do *you* know?

MINOO
The mothers tell me.

Parvez looks at them both in exasperation as she ushers him out of the room.

PARVEZ
How long have you known this?

She looks at him.

I am made into ignoramus. Why?

MINOO
He has had many things to take in. What world are you living in? You don't notice us.

PARVEZ
(*devastated*)
I am nowhere else. After everything, don't I satisfy you?

MINOO
It is you . . . never satisfied with what we do.

Minoo looks at him.

A desperate Parvez watches Farid, who has moved towards the door, having picked up the last box.

PARVEZ'S HOUSE: LIVING ROOM – DAY

Parvez in the front room with a drink, standing at the window watching Farid get into a car driven by one of the young Acolytes we will see later.

INT. CELLAR IN PARVEZ'S HOUSE – DAY

Parvez sits in the cellar – this is his private domain – surrounded by wine and beer-making kits, tools, old newspapers and records.

He takes the piece of paper on which Bettina has written the names of the drugs, and drawn pictures of different kinds of pills, a joint, etc., and looks at it. Then he screws it up and places it beside the screwed-up picture of Madelaine.

Parvez hears Farid enter the house and go up to his room.

Parvez is listening to Louis Armstrong, but after a short time he becomes aware of a new sound. He switches the record off and listens.

INT. THE STAIRWELL OF PARVEZ'S HOUSE – DAY

Parvez emerges from the cellar and heads upstairs, following the sound.

INT. OUTSIDE FARID'S BEDROOM – DAY

Farid's bedroom door is slightly ajar and through the crack Parvez sees his son praying.

On the wall has appeared a gilt framed picture of the Kaaba.

41

INT./EXT. CAB – NIGHT

Parvez driving. Parvez's face, as he attempts to take in what has befallen him.

The illuminated 'Taxi' sign on the roof has developed a fault and flickers on and off. Parvez thumps the ceiling occasionally to try and make it work properly.

INT./EXT. PROSTITUTES' STREET – NIGHT

He enters the 'street of prostitutes' and slows down beside the women. He speaks to a young prostitute – Margot.

> PARVEZ
> Hey, Margot, seen Bettina?

> MARGOT
> Not tonight.

> PARVEZ
> (*to another Woman*)
> Where is she?

> WOMAN
> She's been lucky.

The Controller's voice comes on the radio.

> CONTROLLER
> Your foreigner friend's asking for only you at the Atlantic.
> (*in Punjabi, subtitled*)
> He's giving me a hard time. Please hurry . . . get moving.

Parvez hurriedly turns the car round.

EXT./INT. HOTEL. LATER THAT NIGHT

Parvez has parked outside the German's hotel.

INT. HOTEL

Already late, he hurries in, out of breath, straightening his tie, brushing his hair. The German is at the desk, talking to the Concierge. He turns and sees Parvez.

PARVEZ

Sorry, sorry, four minutes only held up.

GERMAN
(*cheerfully*)
Tonight, little man, we are accompanied.

Parvez doesn't quite understand the German. He turns away and sees a smartly dressed Woman coming down the stairs.

She's wearing the finest cotton, cashmere, satin and silk.
Don't you just love the sound of silk on skin. Her boots are
shining. Puss in Boots I'm calling her now.

Parvez looks at her again, and wonders why she's smiling at him. He recognizes Bettina, wearing a wig.

Pulling himself together, Parvez hurries away to hold the door for them.

There in the lobby the German looks Bettina over, brushes her coat, adjusts her hair, before walking out with her. Parvez then rushes to the car to hold open the doors.

As they get in:

BETTINA
(*whispers to Parvez*)
Looks like I've got the 'shits'.
(*she imitates his accent*)
We are going to look around the place, Puss in Boots.

The German overhears this and is amused.

INT. CAR – EVENING

A hand going up a skirt to pinch a plump thigh.

Parvez driving; the German in the back with his arm around Bettina. Parvez watches them in the rear-view mirror.

PARVEZ
Why come to our town, sir?

GERMAN
Ten years I worked in Munich, Lyon, Bologna. I wanted to

try a strange and awful place where everything was new to me.

> **BETTINA**
>
> How is it?

> **GERMAN**
>
> We will see. Tonight, we will experience some Northern English culture?

> **BETTINA**
>
> We'll be in bed by nine, then.

> **GERMAN**
>
> Come along, Parvez, you join us.

> **PARVEZ**
>
> Oh no, sir.

> **GERMAN**
>
> I book you for the whole evening, little man.

> **BETTINA**
>
> That's right, you've got no choice.

INT. CLUB – EVENING

The German, Bettina and Parvez go down the stairs of the club. One Bouncer stares lasciviously at Bettina. The other Bouncer attempts to bar Parvez's way.

> **GERMAN**
>
> He looks after me.

He slips the Bouncer some money.

> Come, friends.

INT. CLUB – EVENING

The open mouth of a comedian.

The smoky club is packed with raucous drinking men and women. On stage a fat vulgar Comedian is telling a stream of coarse jokes – lesbians, mothers-in-law, etc.

Bettina, the German and Parvez are sitting together at a table. Clearly the German can't follow the Comedian and he leans over Bettina.

GERMAN
Explain me his gist!

Bettina attempts to explain. The German throws his head back and laughs.

Parvez isn't paying much attention to the comedian.

While the German talks into one of Bettina's ears, asking her to explain what is going on – and she attempts some kind of translation – Parvez talks into the other.

PARVEZ
. . . Bettina, you've no idea how relieved I am that the weight of drugs has gone from my head. But why has he never discussed this new direction with me?

BETTINA
(*touching him*)
We all need something to hold on to, don't we?

Parvez considers this.

You must have it out with him.

CUT TO:

Suddenly the spotlight is on Parvez's face, and the Comedian is telling Paki, Rushdie and Muslim jokes. Parvez realizes everyone is turning to look at him, laughing and jeering. He is the only brown face there. He looks at the hostile faces, confused.

As the Comedian addresses him directly the German patronizingly puts his arm around Parvez. Bettina refuses to laugh and looks disgusted.

At the next table a white man has picked up a bread roll and is about to lob it at Parvez. Bettina throws a glass of beer over him. Everyone freezes. The Bouncers move towards them.

The spotlight moves from Parvez's face, the Comedian starts on another joke and the atmosphere changes.

Bettina gets up. She takes Parvez's arm and is about to walk out.

> BETTINA
> (*to German*)

Coming?

> GERMAN
> (*getting up*)

I like a plucky girl.

He ushers Parvez and Bettina out past the Bouncers who stand between them and the crowd. As they go he looks at the hostile faces around them.

And this is the celebrated Northern culture?

EXT. OUTSIDE PUB – NIGHT

Parvez, Bettina and the German hurry across the car park to the car. Rough white men stand at the back-door of the club watching them, whistling and jeering. The German enjoys the exhilaration.

> GERMAN

I will inform the police of this disgust.

BETTINA

They were sitting at the next table.

(*to Parvez*)

You all right?

INT. CAR – NIGHT

Parvez drives off as fast as he can, looking around to see if they've been pursued.

INT. HOTEL CORRIDOR – NIGHT

A lift door opens on Parvez's face. For a moment he stands there unaware of where he is.

Then he struggles up the hotel corridor with bottles of champagne, beer and water, his arms full of crisps and cigarettes.

Pushes the door and goes in.

INT. HOTEL ROOM – NIGHT

Parvez brings the stuff into the room and looks for a place to put it. Music is playing.

Bettina has one foot up on the table, with her dress pulled up, her boot on.

GERMAN

(*to Parvez, checking the bottles*)

Ah, good.

The German sees Parvez glancing at Bettina and smiles, before resuming cutting out a few lines of coke.

GERMAN

Now bring here the dark younger pussy I saw just now on the corner.

PARVEZ

Margot? What for?

GERMAN

To sing to me.

PARVEZ

Can't Bettina sing?

GERMAN

Her voice is too deep.

BETTINA

Your pockets better be.

GERMAN

Here Puss, Puss, Puss.

She laughs.

PARVEZ

Behind the wheel is my racket.

GERMAN

Haven't the people here got no ambition? The Puss want to work, but I thought you immigrants were busy too.

PARVEZ

Sir, where has it got us, and how many of us are happy here?

GERMAN

I feel sorry for you people, I really do.

48

The German looks at him, turns up the music, and nods at Bettina. She comes over and snorts her line. Parvez looks very uncertain; he isn't sure what they're doing. The German indicates that Parvez should try. Parvez looks at Bettina.

PARVEZ

What is it?

BETTINA

It's good coke.

PARVEZ

A drug?

GERMAN

Thank God there's something good in this town.

BETTINA
(*to the German*)
Not since you arrived.
(*shrugs; to Parvez*)
After a certain age there's no point in saying no to everything.

Parvez looks confused. Bettina smiles and goes into the bathroom.

The German indicates for Parvez to open the champagne – three glasses. Then he joins him across the room, out of Bettina's earshot, and speaks to him in a low voice.

GERMAN

For you there's a good drink.

He gives him some money. Parvez pockets it gratefully.

Enjoy yourself with Bettina when I've finished. I see how you look at her. She is delicate, isn't she? How all the parts of women sing out.
(*pause*)
Run along, little man, and bring the dark beauty for double fun! The quality of pussy is not strained, it falleth from street corners like sweet rain.
(*beat*)
My English is even better than yours!

He gives Parvez more money. Then his towel slips. The German ostentatiously removes it and we see he is wearing underneath a pair of silk French knickers. As Parvez looks at him in surprise, the German winks and whistles a happy German song, if there is one.

CUT TO:

At the door Parvez turns and sees Bettina come out of the bathroom, wearing her long overcoat, stockings, boots. The German goes to her, wiggling his arse.

Parvez stands for a moment looking at them, before forcing himself to get out.

EXT. STREET OF PROSTITUTES –NIGHT

Parvez jumps out of his car near the young black prostitute, Margot, who is just about to get into another car.

PARVEZ
Can you sing?

MARGOT
That's one thing no one's asked me to do.

PARVEZ
Get in – Bettina waiting. Good job.

She first has to get rid of the first, now rather angry, driver, who gesticulates violently at Parvez, and gets into Parvez's car.

MARGOT
I didn't know you –

PARVEZ
Favour only.

MARGOT
Long as the ponces don't find out.

Parvez looks nervously at her. She laughs.

EXT. STREET OUTSIDE HOTEL – NIGHT

Parvez under a lamp-post attempting to mend the 'Taxi' light on the roof of his car. He reaches in through the window and throws the switch.

The light flickers. Parvez thumps the fitting: sparks fly, there's a bang, the light dies.

He steps back and looks up at the lighted windows of the hotel, wondering what is going on in there.

CUT TO:

Bettina and Margot skip out of the hotel. Margot sticks her head in the cab window and ruffles Parvez's hair.

MARGOT
Thanks for the work, Parvez.
                    (*to Bettina*)
Coming?

Bettina shakes her head. Margot nods approvingly and walks off in the other direction.

CUT TO:

In the cab Bettina waves money at Parvez.

BETTINA
We are doing very well in Europe. I am all for the Union. Next stop Maastricht!

EXT. OUTSIDE A ROW OF HOUSES – NIGHT

Parvez has parked. Bettina is getting out.

BETTINA
Thanks for helping me out.

He nods. On his face as he watches her go into the house.

CUT TO:

He is about to drive away. Suddenly he changes his mind, gets out and hurries after her. Then he is standing in front of the row of houses, unsure of which is hers.

PARVEZ
(*shouts*)

Bettina! Bettina!

A moment on his face as he waits.

INT. BETTINA'S HOUSE – EARLY MORNING

As Bettina prepares food in the kitchen Parvez is in the living room, looking around, more nervous and uncertain than he is in the cab.

INT. BETTINA'S LIVING ROOM – EARLY MORNING

Bettina is not well-off, but the small flat is neat and cosy. Photographs of her children on the sideboard; ornaments and knick-knacks everywhere.

For the first time we see her without wig or make-up. She wears jeans and a sweatshirt. Classical music is playing.

Parvez stands at the door watching her, looking at her hands, face, as she works, hums and sings a little.

> PARVEZ
> We were only little kids when we came. And the second we stepped from the boat we never stopped working for our families here. Over twenty-five years passed away. I never saw my mother's face again! How I miss them, my parents, and they've been dead all this time! What I would give to see their faces now, for just one minute! But my father was very cruel, and I have tried to love the boy . . .

Tearfully he turns away.

CUT TO:

Later. They are eating breakfast together.

> Thing is, my father used to send me for instruction with the Maulvi – the religious man. But the teacher had this bloody funny effect; whenever he started to speak or read I would fall dead asleep – bang!

Parvez illustrates this narcoleptic state, with snores, impersonating also the Maulvi's monotonous voice.

> Naturally I also annoyed him by asking why my best friend, a Hindu, would go to Kaffir hell when he was such a good chap. His eyes would bulge fully out.

He illustrates.

So he would clip my arms and legs with a cane – like this.
Tuck, tuck – until the blood came!

Parvez illustrates.

But it took no effect. Still I would drop off. He selected
another solution.

BETTINA

Yes?

PARVEZ

He took a piece of string and tied it from the ceiling to my
hair – here. When I dropped off I would wake up – like thus!

His head starts up.

After such treatment I said goodbye permanently to the next
life and said hello to – to work.

BETTINA

Who can blame the young for believing in something beside
money? They are puzzled why a few people have everything
and the poor must sell their bodies. It is positive, in some
ways.

But Parvez looks gloomy.

There is one thing you can try. Give him a better philosophy.

PARVEZ

What type?

BETTINA

How do you feel about things? The purpose of life, and all
that. How should we treat each other?

PARVEZ

Good, I think. Where possible. But I cannot explain the
origin of the universe.

BETTINA

Leave that till later.

INT. BETTINA'S HOUSE, HALLWAY – MORNING

A little later. Bettina and Parvez at the door.

> PARVEZ
> I am full. See you tomorrow.

> BETTINA
> Call me Sandra – when we are alone.

> PARVEZ
> That is the password, eh? To you.

She kisses him on the cheek and then on the mouth. He is surprised.

> BETTINA
> I don't know when I last kissed a man. Sorry. Do you mind?

INT./EXT. CAR/STREET – MORNING

Parvez drives through the deserted streets – a strange, unreal atmosphere – listening to music on the radio, touching his face with his hand, as if to feel her kiss on him.

We see an old bearded Pakistani sitting in the back. They pass the young prostitute, Margot, on the street – running towards a car – and the old man spits and curses in Urdu.

Parvez picks up Bettina's comb from the dashboard and puts it to his face.

BEDROOM. PARVEZ'S HOUSE – MORNING

Parvez is coming out of his bedroom, unshaven, with his hair standing up. (In bed he wears salwar kamiz.)

INT. HALL. PARVEZ'S HOUSE – MORNING

He sees, further down the hall, Minoo, with a tray of drinks and snacks going into Farid's room – backwards with her head bowed and covered.

She looks up and sees Parvez.

PARVEZ

Is he still home?

MINOO

Farid is busy.

Parvez flinches with annoyance, moves past her and goes to the door. Without knocking he goes into Farid's room.

INT. LIVING ROOM. PARVEZ'S HOUSE – MORNING

Five bearded earnest young men in white salwar are sitting in a circle on the floor. In the centre is a tablecloth with tea and biscuits on it. Some of the men lie back; one smokes a pipe. Another is in a wheelchair.

They're reading aloud passages from the Koran and discussing their meaning and relevance. Parvez watches this.

He murmurs some words from the Koran.

He indicates to Farid. At first Farid tries to ignore him. Parvez irritably repeats his gesture.

PARVEZ
I've informed Fizzy we're going tonight to his place.

FARID

Tonight there is a meeting for some friends.

PARVEZ

Isn't it written that you will respect your father?

Farid gives a little nod of reluctant assent. Parvez is pleased with this move.

CUT TO:

Outside Parvez stands there a moment, ear at the door, listening to the murmuring voices.

EXT. STREET – DAY

In his car Parvez has been waiting in a nearby street for the group to leave the house. Some of them split off, but he follows the main group, with Farid.

EXT. STREET OUTSIDE MOSQUE – DAY

They have arrived, with Parvez following, at the mosque. A group of young men, in salwar kamiz, have gathered outside.

Farid has just joined them. They shake hands, embrace and greet each other enthusiastically, before going in.

EXT./INT. MOSQUE – DAY

Parvez, following his son, hurries into the entrance of the mosque. It's been so long since he's done this that he forgets to remove his shoes.

A man takes Parvez's arm and points down at his feet. Parvez takes off his shoes and stands holding them in holed socks, looking around at the numerous faces and different types of people, concealing himself behind a pillar.

Farid's group are entering a room at the far end of the mosque, but as they go in there is an altercation with a older group of men, who try to prevent them going in. Raised voices.

Parvez addresses a man in a Post Office uniform.

> PARVEZ

What's doing here?

> MAN

These boys are not welcome. They are always arguing with the elders. They think everyone but them is corrupt and foolish.

> PARVEZ

What do they want?

> MAN

They are always fighting for radical actions on many subjects. It is irritating us all here, yaar. But they have something these young people – they're not afraid of the truth. They stand up for things. We never did that.

The boys finally gain access to the room, and go in.

Parvez stands there alone. For a moment he looks around and considers praying, but decides not to. And leaves.

INT. PARVEZ IN HIS CUBBY HOLE – EVENING

With a shaking hand, Parvez takes one of his favourite records out of its sleeve and puts it on the deck.

INT. CUBBY HOLE DOOR. PARVEZ'S HOUSE – EVENING

He sticks his head around the door and sees Farid has come downstairs.

INT. CUBBY HOLE. PARVEZ'S HOUSE – EVENING

Parvez puts the record on as Farid comes past the door.

Parvez has dressed up, in an old suit and dismal tie, and has combed his hair. He is nervous and drinking to give himself courage.

> PARVEZ
> (*doing a little dance*)

I'll tape this for you.
> (*pause*)

Or did you sell the player?

As Parvez takes a last swig of his drink, Farid leaves.

Minoo, who has obviously been hovering, goes to Parvez hopefully. He smiles at her, and burps.

> MINOO
> But you are drinking already!

He pushes past her.

> I'll be waiting. Papu, I have such hopes for this evening.

She watches him go.

EXT./INT. FIZZY'S RESTAURANT – NIGHT

As Farid and Parvez walk up to and enter the restaurant Parvez straightens his tie and looks critically at Farid, as if he were a schoolboy; he even reaches out and attempts to brush his hair. Farid moves away in annoyance.

> PARVEZ
> It has been so long since we had a real enjoyable chatterbox!
> (*indicates front of restaurant*)
> What a magnificent joint! Bloody old Fizzy has done good.

INT. FIZZY'S RESTAURANT – NIGHT

As they go in:

> FIZZY
> (*approaching them with two glasses of champagne*)
> What a handsome big man he has grown into! Is he good?

Farid waves away the champagne as Parvez drinks his.

> PARVEZ
> (*into Fizzy's ear*)
> Lately he has been having some funny ideas we must straighten out!

> FIZZY
> And with engagement party coming up. Come – see the room.

Parvez and Farid are reluctant to move.

INT. FUNCTION ROOM – NIGHT

Fizzy, smoking a cigar and sipping champagne, has been, once more, pointing out the qualities of the room.

FIZZY

And over there the beautiful couple will come in, and here we can arrange for . . .

Parvez and Farid stand there, unable to look at each other or speak. Fizzy's flow isn't stemmed by their embarrassment.

PARVEZ
(*whispers*)
Have you really made up your mind about this thing.

FARID

She is absolutely not right for me. But perhaps for you . . .

PARVEZ

You are becoming very disrespectful. I can still clip your ear.

Fizzy turns and sees them arguing.

INT. KITCHEN – NIGHT

Fizzy has taken Parvez and Farid into the kitchen, introduced him to the Chef and is proudly showing them the kitchen equipment.

The Chef stuffs a big white napkin into Parvez's collar: it remains there until they leave the restaurant. Meanwhile the Chef has Parvez try all the dishes, holding the spoon to his mouth.

FIZZY

Many thanks, yaar, for the German. Those Krauts certainly stuff themselves up.

As the Chef leads him around the kitchen Parvez swoons enthusiastically at each mouthful, until he is practically fainting in appreciation.

PARVEZ
Again tasty! Extra tasty! More tasty!

Fizzy goes to Farid.

FIZZY

On our last day there his mother made me promise to look
after him. You must cherish your father.

FARID

Fizzy, uncle, haven't we lost our way here?

FIZZY

What? Some of us are doing real good.

FARID

Even so, we lack something inside.

FIZZY

Leave that crap to the old men, yaar. We are getting on.

Parvez looks over at him.

(*to Farid*)

Good boy, eh?

INT. THE RESTAURANT – EVENING

*Parvez sits down opposite his son and indicates the restaurant, smiling
at people at other tables.*

PARVEZ
(*indicating the place*)

Bloody old Fizzy. But as your mother correctly confirms
independently, he is greedy and all.

*Fizzy comes over with two large glasses of whisky which he puts down
in front of each of them. Parvez is a little embarrassed, since he
imagines Fizzy might have overheard his last words.*

FIZZY

Tonight you drink and eat as my guest!

PARVEZ

No. Fizzy –

FIZZY

Without a quibble! Wedding present, yaar!

Fizzy bows and leaves them. Parvez adjusts his napkin and takes a long drink of whisky. Farid pushes away his own glass.

> PARVEZ

If I'd know it was free I would have missed lunch!

He leans forward and says confidently:

> I tell everyone, eat here and you'll never be constipated again!

The Waiter comes over with plates.

> WAITER

We will bring a good selection.

> PARVEZ

This is my only son.

> (*to Farid*)

Have a beer with dad.

Farid shakes his head, and the waiter goes.

> FARID

Don't you know it's wrong to drink alcohol?

Farid is looking at him steadily. Parvez bangs his glass down on the table and laughs dismissively.

> It is forbidden. Gambling too.

> PARVEZ

I am a man.

> FARID

You have the choice, then, to do good or evil.

> PARVEZ

I may be weak and foolish, but please inform me, am I really, according to you, wicked?

> FARID

If you break the law as stated then how can wickedness not follow? You eat the pig. In the house.

> PARVEZ

A bacon butty? Tasty! You loved them too.

FARID
(*a little shiftily*)
Perhaps. I didn't force mother to eat it.

PARVEZ
(*laughs*)
Force – her lips were twitching!
(*pause*)
In the days of the Prophet the pig was contaminated meat.
Farid, this purity interest. What is it about?

FARID
Who in this country could not want purity?

A Waiter brings a tray of various foods. Parvez looks at it with enthusiasm.

PARVEZ
Good man!
(*to Farid*)
Try that. Or this! Delicious.

He leans towards Farid and says confidently:

Seriously, these English, you'd be a fool to run them down –

FARID
I have been thinking seriously.

PARVEZ
Good.

FARID
They say integrate, but they live in pornography and filth, and tell us how backward we are!

PARVEZ
There's no doubt, compared to us, they can have funny habits and all –

FARID
A society soaked in sex –

PARVEZ

(*eating*)

Not that I've benefited! Where do you think the drugs come
from? It is Rashid's relatives sending them, yaar! Anyhow,
how else can we belong here except by mixing up all together?
They accuse us of keeping with each other.

FARID

Yes!

PARVEZ

But I invite the English. Come – share my food! And all the
years I've lived here, not one single Englishman has invited
me to his house – apart from Fingerhut, who is a top-class
gentleman! But still I make the effort.

FARID

You see, we have our own system. It is useless to grovel to the
whites!

PARVEZ

Grovel!

FARID

It sickens me to see you lacking pride.

PARVEZ

Fill up for two days.

FARID

Thing is, you are too implicated in Western civilization.

PARVEZ

Implicated!

*He stares at his son and burps. The Waiter is hovering by the table. To
him:*

You hear what clever words my boy is using against me?
Implicated!

Waiter goes.

FARID

Whatever we do here we will always be inferior. They will

never accept us as like them. But I am not inferior! Don't they patronize and insult us? How many times have they beaten you?

PARVEZ

With my cricket bat I have always defended without fear!

FARID

How can you say they're not devils?

PARVEZ

Not everyone, I am saying! Farid, this is not the village but our home country, we have to get along. Tell me something useful, boy. Is it true you don't love Madelaine?

FARID

What is that kind of love? Here all the marriages last five minutes. Respect and devotion is better. Are you in love?

PARVEZ

I'm beginning to see what it is. There is curiosity. Fascination. The feeling that the other person is . . . more important than anyone else. And it is . . .

FARID

Lately you've become very introspective.

PARVEZ

I found something . . . an airline ticket, you know, in your room.

FARID

What were you doing in there?

PARVEZ
(*with a mouthful of food*)
Eh? A little dusting.

Farid can't help himself – he laughs. A moment of spontaneity.

FARID

Why snoop around?

PARVEZ

What is the ticket for?

FARID

Papa, I want you to do something for me.

PARVEZ

Have I ever refused you one thing?

FARID

Papa, there is a wise maulvi from Lahore. He is a good man
and we have invited him to offer us a little instruction. Can't
he stay a few days?

*Without thinking, Parvez picks up his whisky and drinks, waving his
drink approvingly at a Waiter.*

PARVEZ

In our house?

FARID
(*excessively polite*)

If you would give permission.

*Farid sees Parvez give a little confused and perfunctory nod. The
waiters bring more food and drink. Parvez's mouth is messy with food,
and he drops keema and dall on to his trousers.*

PARVEZ

That is what the money was for? You're not going anywhere?

FARID
(*shaking his head*)

He can stay?

PARVEZ
(*nods*)

Our house is open. Why haven't you told me about this
interest?

FARID
(*shifty*)

The irreligious find belief difficult to comprehend. Those
who love the sacred are called fundamentalists, terrorists,
fanatics.

PARVEZ

And this is why you've left Madelaine? Her father, Chief
Inspector Fingerhut of the police force –

FARID
(*sighing*)

Papa –

PARVEZ

I don't want this anti-Fingerhut face!

FARID

But you are reminding me of something disgusting! Surely
you grasped how ashamed I was, seeing you toadying to
Fingerhut.

Parvez stares at him, a handful of chapati at his mouth.

FARID

The girl is okay. But Fingerhut . . . Do you think his men
care about racial attacks? And couldn't you see how much he
hated his daughter being with me, and how . . . repellent he
found you? I never want to see those people again.

*Parvez is in shock, drinking, shaking his head to clear his brain, and
looking around the restaurant, as if for assistance. He is starting to get
drunk.*

PARVEZ
(*watching Farid*)

All right. If this is reality, that I am disgusting, that I have
never been a good man, and never done anything worthwhile,
I must face it. After all, you have observed me for a long time.
(*pause*)
But tonight I am determined to get one good thing. Tell me
that at least you are keeping up with your studies.

FARID

Papa, there are suffering men in prison who require guidance.

PARVEZ

What guidance? If they're inside they must be fools!

FARID

I have never met men more sincere and thirsty for the spirit.
And accountancy . . . it is just capitalism and taking
advantage. You can never succeed in it unless you go to the
pub and meet women.

*Parvez starts to yell. Customers look around at him. Waiters and Fizzy
stand watching concernedly.*

PARVEZ

Fool, you're beginning to irritate my arse! What's wrong with
women!

FARID

Many lack belief and therefore reason. Papa, the final
Message is a complete guidance –

PARVEZ

You donkey's dirty arse, this evening you have shown only
one thing –

FARID

This is the true alternative to empty living from day to
day . . .

Fizzy rushes over to see what the commotion is.

. . . in the capitalist dominated world we are suffering from! I
am telling you, the Jews and Christers will be routed! You
have taken the wrong side!

PARVEZ

One thing, one thing I know –

FARID

Papa, please, it is not too late! I beg you to seek Allah's
forgiveness for your mistakes!

PARVEZ

Please, boy, don't go too far with this thing!

FARID

No. It is you who have swallowed the white and Jewish
propaganda that there is nothing to our lives but the empty

accountancy of things . . . of things . . . for nothing . . . for nothing.

PARVEZ
I am swallowing nothing but brother Fizzy's dinner, and it will give me indigestion now.

By mistake he sweeps a dish from the table.

But a wasp has gone into your gullet!

Fizzy rushes over to see what the commotion is.

FIZZY
Mayor is sitting over there! Eat!

PARVEZ
I have lost my appetite! The boy is massacring my life!

Parvez is choking and distraught.

EXT. FIZZY'S RESTAURANT – NIGHT

Farid is leading Parvez out.

FIZZY
I've never seen him like this. A drinking taxi-driver is a bloody fool.

FARID
Who gave him the alcohol?

Fizzy stares at Farid. Just then, they run into the German and Bettina coming in, arm-in-arm.

GERMAN
Little man, you are everywhere!

Parvez is unable to stop looking at Bettina, who smiles at him.

BETTINA
(*indicating Farid*)
This is him.

She is about to put out her hand, but stops herself.

The German addresses Parvez.

> GERMAN
>
> I am organizing party, for business acquaintances. Your
> friend here can fix food –

> PARVEZ
>
> Yes, yes.

> GERMAN
>
> But I can leave the girls to you? Diversification, eh? Only the
> best Puss in Boots, like Bettina, eh? Good, good . . .

As the German and Parvez talk, Bettina and Farid are left together.
Bettina is unsure whether to say anything. At last she decides to do so.

> BETTINA
>
> Your father talks about you 'non-stop', as he puts it.

Farid smiles politely.

> Your exams are going well?

Farid nods a bit.

> What will you do later?

> FARID
>
> Something good.

> BETTINA
>
> I hope so.

> FARID
>
> And you?

She looks at him.

> How do you know Dad?

> BETTINA
>
> I see him about.

> FARID
>
> What do you do?

> BETTINA

I am in . . . industry.

Farid looks her up and down. Parvez has seen this. He takes Farid's arm and leads him away.

> CUT TO:

Parvez turns and watches the German put his arm gently around Bettina's waist and leads her down to the door of the restaurant.

EXT. STREET. PARVEZ'S CAB. OUTSIDE RESTAURANT – EVENING

Parvez is attempting, drunkenly to clamber into the driver's seat. He slips and almost falls. Farid tries to manoeuvre him into the back.

Fizzy and a Waiter stand in the doorway of the restaurant, watching with concern.

> FIZZY
> (*shouting to Parvez*)

Rear seat, yaar!

> FARID

Yes, Papa, please –

> PARVEZ

Don't pull! Haven't you destroyed me already?

> FARID

Better not lose your licence too.

Fizzy runs down and helps manoeuvre the flailing Parvez into the back.

INT. CAR – NIGHT

By now Parvez is in the back and Farid is driving.

> FARID
> (*into car radio*)

Papa's clocking off.

> CONTROLLER

Passed any exams today, Farid?

Farid snaps the radio off.

                    PARVEZ
                  (*to Farid*)
You think you're a smart mister, but you are taking us wrong
route!

                    FARID
I will show you something.

                    PARVEZ
Go to hell!

*Farid smiles bitterly to himself – used to this. He drives in another
direction.*

CUT TO:

*A few minutes later. Lying back in the car, Parvez is talking, ignoring
where they're going.*

I know what it is . . . you see, I haven't loved life here apart
from – Farid, I have loved your company, as a baby, and as a
boy. I would get out of bed only to look at your face. For you
it was just growing up. For me the best of life itself.

*Meanwhile Farid picks up, from the dashboard, a lip-stick and comb
belonging to Bettina, and looks curiously at them. Parvez sees this.*

Farid throws them down and turns the car into a housing estate.

INT./EXT. CAR. CONTINUOUS TIME

*Farid drives into a rough part of a nearby run-down estate. Many of
the houses are boarded up, the cars abandoned or burned out; a lawless
atmosphere.*

*A bunch of white and black kids are hanging out under the street lights,
watching one of the gang doing handbrake turns in a stolen car. They're
a wretched bunch, fighting and shoving each other around. Music from
someone's ghetto-blaster. This would be a part of town that Parvez
wouldn't know much about.*

Farid slows down and Parvez sits up to look out.

PARVEZ

Where have you brought us?

Farid gets out.

PARVEZ

Farid!

Parvez, afraid, leans over the seat and pulls out his piece of wood.

Noticing Farid, two older Lads approach him. Seeing they're friendly, Parvez gets out, holding the piece of wood, and maintains himself upright by holding onto the roof.

LAD

Hey, Farid, Farid. Not on the rides like your old man?

Farid shakes his head. Parvez is trying, drunkenly, to present himself respectably, and puts out his hand – transferring the piece of wood clumsily to his other hand.

As the Lads greet him, Parvez is unable to prevent himself from retching and coughing. He eventually straightens up and takes some deep breaths.

What's he on?

Farid looks at Parvez in disgust.

(*to Farid*)

Sorted?

FARID

Got everything I need.

LAD

Lucky lad.

FARID

What you doing?

LAD

Starting fires, yeah.
(*chants*)
Burn it down, burn it down!

74

As Farid chats to the Lads, Parvez, feeling better but requiring fresh air, stands up and walks towards the houses, people and children around him. It is cold and desolate.

CUT TO:

Farid, with the two Lads behind him, has joined Parvez. They stroll around a little until they come to a group of kids playing around a bonfire, and throwing stuff onto it.

PARVEZ

We have come from one Third World country to another.

A little kid comes towards Farid and whispers something in his ear. Farid shakes his head, smiles in a kindly way, shrugs, and sends the boy away.

Those boys are selling the drug.

FARID

I was at school with those lads, until they burned it down.

PARVEZ

They did it? What will happen to them?

FARID

Some will die, or get snuffed. Many will go to prison. The lucky ones stay here, and rot.

PARVEZ

This shows we must –

FARID

I was like them, going to hell in a hurry.

PARVEZ

When?

FARID

Before I learned there could be another way.

PARVEZ

But you were studying.

Farid shrugs.

75

You fooled us.

> FARID

For months I was high and low at the same time, lying on the floor in bloody terrible places. I thought I could never get back.

> PARVEZ

But what of Madelaine? You went to the Chief Inspector's house every night, to study and all.

> FARID

She was the same.

> PARVEZ

Never lie to me!

> FARID

We did everything together.

> PARVEZ

Under his nose? But not now?

> FARID

I have returned from something – clean and serene.

> PARVEZ

Why didn't you tell me?

Farid shrugs.

How could such a thing have happened?

> FARID

Evil is all around. The brothers have given me the strength to save myself. In the midst of corruption there can be purity.

CUT TO:

Retching, Parvez gets back into the car and as he vomits on the back seat:

> PARVEZ
> (*to Farid*)

Oh God, not on new upholstery.

Farid hands him some tissues.

Fizzy's food. Remind me to insist on refund.

INT./EXT. STREET – EVENING

A bit later. The car halts at traffic-lights. On the corner three prostitutes are standing – one of them Margot.

They recognize Parvez in the back of the car, and wave and call out to him.

MARGOT

Give us a lift!

For a moment he smiles, and then, catching Farid's alert eye in the mirror, he turns away, ignoring the girls.

FARID

Filthy women, near the children's school.

PARVEZ

What can be done with human nature, boy?

FARID

Send them away.

PARVEZ

Soon everyone will go away. They're building a shopping centre outside the city where people will buy everything. The small shopkeeper has had his chips. We might as well go home again.

INT. HALLWAY. PARVEZ'S HOUSE – NIGHT

Minoo is waiting when they come back. She opens the door to see Farid and a distressed Parvez. As Parvez gets past them Farid whispers quickly to Minoo.

FARID

I am going ahead with all arrangements.

MINOO

He agreed?

FARID

He is beginning to see things from another point of view.

Minoo looks surprised.

INT. BEDROOM – NIGHT

Parvez is sitting on the edge of the bed. Minoo comes in.

MINOO

Well? Tell me, man. Speak, speak – if you can!

Parvez gestures and waves as if everything is beyond his comprehension. Then, slowly, he starts to move.

PARVEZ

I'm going out . . to work and all, you know, what else?

She shakes her head. He attempts to get up. Then he gives up.

Later, then. Can't you help me?

MINOO

All my life I have helped you.

Impatiently she goes to him and starts undoing his shirt.

PARVEZ

Touch me then, here.

In illustration, he rubs his forehead. She continues with the buttons.

He starts to stroke her; he puts his hand between her legs. She is unresponsive. Parvez opens the front of his trousers.

Minee. Minee, can't you –

She brushes his hands away.

MINOO

Today I am exhausted.

PARVEZ

It must be exhausting, sitting here all day –

MINOO

Shut up, clown.

Suddenly he grabs her and viciously forces her onto the bed.

What are you doing! No, no! Leave me! Leave me! Parvez you have become an animal!

She is not strong, but he is drunk. They continue to struggle, and Parvez is very determined.

Finally she shoves him, and he crashes off the bed and lies there winded. She gets to her feet, shocked, pulling her clothes down.

MINOO
Don't ever do that to me again! I will kill you!

She abuses him in Urdu.

He looks up at her, before rolling over and facing in the other direction.

INT. LIVING ROOM – DAY

Parvez wakes up on the sofa in the living room, hears a noise and heads out into the hall to see what it is.

INT. HALL – DAY

Farid and a couple of his Student friends cleaning the whole house, as quickly and thoroughly as they can.

Farid looks up and smiles at Parvez. Another Student is on his knees scrubbing the hall tiles.

PARVEZ
Don't miss a bit and do my shoes while you're down there.

Minoo struggles through the front door with several shopping bags, accompanied by another Student who is also carrying bags.

Through the open door we see that Parvez's car is being cleaned by a Student.

PARVEZ
Don't scratch my bonnet!
                (*to Farid, who has come out*)
What is this?

FARID

Surely you remember?

EXT. PARVEZ'S HOUSE – DAY

Outside, Rashid's cab draws up and he beeps his horn. Parvez looks confused.

PARVEZ

And that donkey?

FARID

Get dressed, Papa.

INT. HALL. PARVEZ'S HOUSE – DAY

Minoo comes to Parvez and Farid. For Parvez she has freshly cleaned shoes; for Farid the new white salwar.

Parvez looks at them both, conspirators.

EXT. OUTSIDE THE HOUSE, MOMENTS LATER – DAY

On the front path, Farid and Parvez, wearing their new garments, have a sudden heated argument, watched by various others, including Minoo and Rashid.

PARVEZ

Is it what you want, or what they've ordered you to do –

FARID

Papa, you gave your word –

PARVEZ

Put this man in a hotel! The Atlantic, I can get a special price –

FARID

More boasting.

PARVEZ

He'll stir up the pots, you don't know what these religious people are like, imposing mad ideas –

FARID

Papa . . . the people are thirsty, thirsty –

Parvez walks away, towards the car.

PARVEZ

I'm beginning to feel bloody thirsty.

INT./EXT. PARKING AREA. AIRPORT – DAY

Rashid – the spiteful colleague from the taxi firm – is leaning against his cab, picking his teeth. Parvez stands next to him.

RASHID

How long is he putting up in your house?

Parvez glances irritably at him.

Haven't been informed, eh? You are in a good mood.

PARVEZ

Why not, monkey face?

RASHID

You've changed. I wonder why.

PARVEZ

It would be worse to be the same.

Rashid looks up and hastily sprays air-freshener into his car. Parvez puts his paper away and looks up.

The long-bearded Maulvi from Pakistan has arrived. He walks out of the airport surrounded by five or six young men, carrying his luggage – including Farid, who has sponsored him.

The Maulvi is tall and thin, wearing elegant long robes. He is a little effete, and rather self-important. And he is younger than Parvez had imagined.

Rashid and Parvez open the car doors.

INT./EXT. CAR. STREET

The Maulvi is sitting in the back of Parvez's cab with another Student beside him. Farid sits beside Parvez but talks, very respectfully to the Maulvi.

> FARID
>
> That extremely tall chimney on the left perfectly symbolizes the overblown egos of nineteenth-century British industrialists. It was built that high so the smoke from it would blow over the house of one of his rivals.
>
> Actually, Ayatollah Khomeini wore a robe made here. The place where it was manufactured used to be on the right. Unfortunately it was demolished some years ago.

INT.EXT. CAR. PROSTITUTES' STREET

Parvez is amused. He turns the wheel of the car. The Maulvi is looking out of the window. Farid notices that they are driving up the street of prostitutes.

> FARID
> (*whispers to Parvez*)
>
> Wrong way!

> PARVEZ
>
> Let him see true life, yaar!
> (*to the Maulvi*)
> On the right we have –

But on the left are the line of Prostitutes which the Mullah looks at. Parvez sees Bettina and smiles. She waves at him. Farid sees her too, remembering her, of course, from the restaurant.

An Asian family with several children pass the Prostitutes.

> FARID
> (*embarrassedly to the Maulvi*)
> In the West everywhere there is immorality.

> MAULVI
>
> You take no action?

PARVEZ

The wild spice and variety of life is goes on everywhere – like in Lahore, and Karachi. Eh?

And he slaps his son playfully on the knee. Then he turns and gets a good look at the Maulvi.

INT. PARVEZ'S HOUSE – DAY

The Maulvi is looking around Parvez's front room. Everyone holds their breath, awaiting his approval. At last he nods. Minoo in the doorway.

The place is not only preternaturally tidy, but the furniture has been moved around.

With the Maulvi, Parvez looks around quizzically, wondering what has happened.

MAULVI

I will feel as if I am at home.

FARID

We couldn't ask for more.

They sigh with relief.

Parvez stands to one side, looking on with envy and cynical amusement.

INT. KITCHEN. PARVEZ'S HOUSE – DAY

Farid comes out of the kitchen with a tray of food.

INT. DINING ROOM. PARVEZ'S HOUSE – DAY

The Maulvi sits at the table, studying a religious book. Farid puts the food in front of him and sits down opposite.

Parvez comes into the room, sees the Maulvi and looks around uncomfortably, before sitting down. He is about to take a mouthful when he notices the Maulvi is not eating.

PARVEZ

Eat, eat.

Maulvi reaches across for food. He isn't about to make conversation. Parvez, about to tuck in, looks up to see where Minoo is. He notices, then, that no place has been set for her.

> PARVEZ

Where's your mother?

> FARID
> (*uneasily, glancing at the Maulvi*)

Busy in the kitchen, I think.

> PARVEZ
> (*to Maulvi*)

We always eat together as a family, otherwise we would see one another even less.

INT. KITCHEN. PARVEZ'S HOUSE – DAY

Parvez goes into the kitchen to find her eating alone.

> PARVEZ

Come.

She shakes her head. He picks up her plate and takes it to the door.

Come!

INT. LIVING ROOM. PARVEZ'S HOUSE – DAY

He goes into the living room with the plate, puts it down on the table.

I will not eat without you!

The Maulvi remains silent. Minoo has not shifted from the kitchen. Parvez looks at Farid.

INT. KITCHEN. PARVEZ'S HOUSE – DAY

In the kitchen, in front of Minoo, Parvez ostentatiously scrapes the food from his plate into the bin.

INT. CELLAR – DAY

A romantic record is playing; Parvez is wearing just a shirt, new tie, and socks. He has damp hair. Having placed a mirror against a shelf, he is snipping at the hair in his nostrils, ears and eyebrows with a inconveniently large and blunt pair of scissors. He stands back and regards himself.

He hears a noise behind him and turns around nervously.

Minoo comes in with a plate of food and cutlery.

> PARVEZ

You've thrown away my bottle! What am I working for if I can't even wet my mouth!

> MINOO

When you drink you play that music.

> PARVEZ

What's wrong with Louis Armstrong? You don't know.

> MINOO
> (*pause*)

It's too trumpety. Here.

She offers him the food.

> PARVEZ

You eat too.

> MINOO

I am full.

She watches him, as he puts on his trousers.

> PARVEZ
> (*self-conscious*)

German likes me to dress well.
> (*pause*)

I must start getting like Farid and his longbeard best friend – laying down the law for other people. I don't know how you can talk to that man without wanting to give his whiskers a hard tug. I might do it myself – then we'll see what's underneath!

He illustrates.

MINOO
(*stopping a giggle*)

Papu!

PARVEZ

I will tug – so!

CUT TO:

Minoo has gone. Parvez puts 'Mack the Knife' (or similar) on the record-player and opens the door. As he lets the first notes blare out into the house, he laughs to himself. He leans out of the door before the enquiring head of the Maulvi appears at the living room door, followed by Farid's head.

Parvez enjoys the mischief for a moment, before banging a pair of headphones over his head and doing a little dance to the music. He is quite excited.

CUT TO:

INT. HOUSE – EVENING

Parvez tiptoes past the door of the front room where the Mullah, surrounded by Acolytes, is talking.

EXT. STREET – NIGHT

Parvez helps an elegant Bettina out of the car, outside Fizzy's restaurant.

A smart white couple, seeing, of course, that it is a taxi, wave at Parvez, who dismisses them irritably.

PARVEZ

Not for hire or sale! How beautiful you look tonight, my love.

INT. RESTAURANT – EVENING

Tonight it is crowded. Parvez points out Fizzy, who glances over but doesn't immediately respond.

BETTINA

Did you make a booking?

PARVEZ

Silly, Fizzy used to carry my cricket bag. His father –

BETTINA

Why did you want to come here?

PARVEZ

Best place. This is the bloody life, yaar! I am so glad to get out of that house. And Farid says the cultures cannot mix. Jesus, they can't keep apart.

Fizzy comes over, puzzled by Parvez's sartorial care, and by his beaming happiness.

(*to Bettina*)
This is my first-friend – Fizzy.

FIZZY

And who is this friend?

PARVEZ

Bett – Sandra.

FIZZY

Madam.

He takes her hand; to Parvez.

We are fully booked, yaar.

PARVEZ

Fizzy, yaar –

FIZZY

Okay, okay. Upstairs everything is good.

As the Waiter leads them away:

Where have I seen that tart?

WAITER

She came with the German who ate the whole kitchen and then said it was too salty.

Fizzy watches and nods.

CUT TO:

INT. FUNCTION ROOM. RESTAURANT. CONTINUOUS

One Waiter carries a table over; another lays it.

Parvez and Bettina are now sitting down – in the room previously visited. It is a big room with only a few tables, and less people eating. It is far less salubrious than downstairs, and Parvez is taken aback that his friend has done this to him.

CUT TO:

Parvez chatting away, trying to make the best of it.

> PARVEZ
> You can't force anyone to be sensible.

> BETTINA
> I made a resolution – to try something new every day. I've even signed up for evening classes.

> PARVEZ
> In what?

> BETTINA
> Singing.

> PARVEZ
> Singing? Good idea. In school I loved the hymns. One thing I regret. Farid wanted to study music and arts and all . . . and I didn't listen, but forced him into science and maths. It caused a resentment.
> > (*pause*)
> You were telling me, that thing about your mother and –

> BETTINA
> Well, she –

She looks up and Parvez is stuffing his face with food. She laughs. He looks quizzically at her.

> BETTINA
> You look like a hamster.

I'm not used to being looked at with curiosity.

BETTINA

Nor me, really.

They look at one another, as if trying to work something out.

When you meet a new person you don't know where you are. There is . . . possibility.

They are both feeling awkward.

Why did you come here?

PARVEZ

To feed my family only. I never saw further. You have been a dreamer?

BETTINA

I wanted to be a teacher. But my children were too young. Then my man died and I had debts. I had a friend who was doing this. If you had the choice what would you do?

PARVEZ

It's been so long since I have thought about anything.

Fizzy comes over.

FIZZY

What is date for engagement booking?

PARVEZ
(*looking at Bettina*)

At this moment, Fizzy brother, I am completely engaged and booked elsewhere.

FIZZY
(*banging his fist on the table*)

Parvez, yaar –

Parvez quickly leads him away from the table. Fizzy is furious.

PARVEZ

Whole question of engagement is off, yaar, for time being, at the moment, for now –

What?

PARVEZ

I am stuffed up, far into rear end. The boy doesn't like the
girl. The girl is fighting with –

FIZZY

You are giving Fingerhut the finger! But we were expecting
community policing at last.

Parvez notices that Fizzy is looking quizzically at him.

What's happened to your eyebrows?

*Fizzy looks over at Bettina and is about to say something, but Parvez
moves away from Fizzy and sits down again.*

Bettina seems agitated. She gets up.

BETTINA

Sorry, I can't stay.

*She walks out. Parvez gets up and watches her go, not knowing what to
do. At that moment a Waiter brings the food.*

INT./EXT. RESTAURANT – NIGHT

*Fizzy at the window. He watches an anxious Parvez run to Bettina
and take her arm. She puts her arm around him.*

INT. BETTINA'S HOUSE – NIGHT

*Bettina is getting changed in the bedroom. Parvez watches her through
the open door. He sees that new clothes are hanging from door handles
and the tops of doors.*

PARVEZ

All that is new?

BETTINA

The big Shit is paying.

PARVEZ

You're seeing him often.

Saves me seeing anyone else.

PARVEZ

You don't . . . talk to him.

BETTINA

That's not what he wants.

He glimpses a bruise on her forearm.

PARVEZ

That him, too?

BETTINA

I think I look excellent. If you don't like it, you can go. Go
on.
(*beat*)
You like me today don't you? Sometimes you're not so sure.
Do you know why you like me?

PARVEZ

It's only that I can't help thinking that you are a magnificent,
special woman. It's a feeling I want to push away. It makes
me feel good, and as if I'm going mad.

BETTINA

You know what I've always wanted to do?

*She puts her hand in his hair and tugs it, quite hard. He winces and
smiles.*

Does your wife do that?

PARVEZ

Why are you asking?

BETTINA

It's something I can't help thinking about.

PARVEZ

She's too bloody ugly.

*Bettina laughs. Parvez is horrified by what he has said. She stands in
the doorway of her bedroom.*

CUT TO:

Parvez and Bettina standing by her bedroom door, not together.

BETTINA
I lie in bed with the music on. When I think of you I get a warm feeling in my stomach and I have to close my eyes. No other man has come in here.

CUT TO:

Bettina's face. Parvez's hands on her face. He caresses her forehead, eyes, mouth, exploring.

CUT TO:

She examines the palms of his hands and his fingers; kisses them.

She kisses her own hands and rubs them over his face.

Hands; lips; kisses; bits of body.

INT. PARVEZ'S HOUSE. CELLAR – NIGHT

Parvez's trembling fingers unbuttoning his shirt.

He has come home at last. He removes his shirt, burying his face in her scent. He changes into another shirt, crumpled up on the side, doing up the buttons wrong.

INT. PARVEZ'S HOUSE – BEDROOM

Upstairs. Parvez is going to bed, exhausted. Minoo is standing in front of him. Parvez looks at her guiltily.

He moves past her and turns the corner on the upper landing. He sees Farid sleeping outside his own bedroom. Taken aback, he steps over him, opens the bedroom door, and sees and hears the snoring Maulvi in his son's bed.

PARVEZ
These people are even taking over our beds.

Minoo puts her finger to her lips. Parvez shakes his head in disbelief and goes past.

IN. PARVEZ'S HOUSE. KITCHEN – DAY

In the kitchen the Maulvi is having breakfast watching cartoons on TV. Farid is in the room waiting on him. Parvez comes in, dressed, and ready for work.

PARVEZ
(*sarcastically*)

What can I get you?

The Maulvi continues to watch TV. Finally he looks at Parvez and gives a little shiver.

MAULVI

To be honest . . . I am a little chilly.

Minoo rushes in from the kitchen.

MINOO

Chilly?

(*to Farid*)

He's chilly.

FARID

Chilly?

Minoo looks around, spots a blanket lying on the back of a chair, and puts it over the Maulvi's legs. The Maulvi sighs contentedly. They look at him. He gives another little shiver.

I'll get the fan-heater!

Farid goes to leave, rushing out but returning immediately. Parvez looks on incredulously.

FARID
(*to Minoo*)

Where is it? The heater!

She rushes out of the room to help Farid.

Hearing the phone ring, Parvez goes, shaking his head.

INT. PARVEZ'S HOUSE. HALL – DAY

Parvez on the phone in the hall.

PARVEZ
(*whispers urgently into phone*)
Herr Schitz, Herr Schitz, I am only driver but am arranging
everything with red-hot tarts toot suite. I know where it is, yes.

As he speaks Minoo rushes past with the heater.

INT. CAB OFFICE – DAY

*Parvez arrives at the cab office. As he hurries through the entrance he
finds the addict Prostitute coming at him.*

PROSTITUTE
Parvez, are you going my way? I know you are –

*He brushes past her. Looks over at another Driver. As the Prostitute
turns back to him, he shakes his head, also refusing to take her. She is
too out of it.*

DRIVER
You girls are going to be in bloody big trouble. 'Bout time
too!

PROSTITUTE
You men are a load of hypocrites!

CAB CONTROLLER
How's things at home? The boy.

Parvez shakes his head.

PARVEZ
I need a couple of drivers to help me out later.

CAB CONTROLLER
See who's around.

INT. TAXI OFFICE – DAY

Parvez comes into the main taxi office.

*Across the room, Rashid has clearly been gossiping with the Cab
Controller and other Drivers about the just-arrived Maulvi. Some nod
gravely, others smirk and laugh, others look on. But everybody knows,
and has an opinion.*

On the video in the corner a porn film is playing. One of the Drivers stands in front of it mockingly to prevent Parvez from seeing it.

Parvez looks at Rashid reproachfully, and at the others, and sighs.

Then he notices that two of the Drivers are playing cricket with a rolled-up ball of paper and bat. Parvez does a double-take at the bat and grabs it.

DRIVER

Signed by Imran. Open the batting, yaar.

Thinking Parvez wants to play, the Driver hands him the bat. Parvez examines it. It is the bat from Farid's room, signed by the Pakistan cricket team.

PARVEZ

Where did you find this?

DRIVER

My boy.

PARVEZ

It's not his.

DRIVER

Your son sold it.

DRIVER 2

How's your new lodger, yaar?

DRIVER 3

Given up all your bad vices? No more bacon butties!

DRIVER 2

They say you can't even get a drink in your place now. Is it true you're living under stairs like a troll?

DRIVER 3

The Ayatollah's moving in permanently, has he?

DRIVER

These demonstrations he has in mind are starting, they say. It's a bloody nuisance and all, affecting our work.

RASHID

They are vile girls! There is too much unbelieving going on.
Everywhere there is evil to be cured. Parvez has right idea!

*Parvez opens his wallet and contemptuously throws money at the Driver
from whom he's snatched the bat.*

*A Driver stands in front of him, smirking. Parvez pushes past him and
raises his hand as if to hit him.*

Behind him the Drivers laugh.

CUT TO:

Parvez is leaving the outer office, carrying the cricket bat.

PARVEZ

I am on urgent business. Tonight, later, I will work. But you
must get me two drivers.

CONTROLLER

Taking your girlfriend somewhere nice?

PARVEZ

Girlfriend?

CONTROLLER

What name she use?

Parvez looks blank.

Bettina? Everybody says –

PARVEZ

Everybody says nothing – bloody fool!

Parvez rushes out.

EXT. STREET – DAY

Parvez drives up the street of prostitutes towards Margot.

Along the street a Brother is tying a poster to a tree.

*Further along the Maulvi, Farid and a couple of other Brothers
standing on a corner watching the proceedings, and talking
concentratedly with one another.*

He backs the car off a little in order to watch them without being observed himself.

A Punter in a car approaches one of the Women. Farid ostentatiously brandishes a notebook and writes down his registration number.

The car drives off.

The Woman abuses Farid. He abuses her back.

> FARID
> Get out of here, you filthy women!

Parvez looks on. Finally he turns the car round. We see that Farid has looked up and noticed his father's car.

> CAB CONTROLLER
> Parvez, the boys are ready!

INT. CAR – EVENING

> CUT TO: *a Prostitute making up her face.*

A harassed Parvez has, in his car, three of the more salubrious Prostitutes, who have dressed up for the occasion, and Margot.

> CUT TO:

Parvez is driving them towards the mill we have already seen. The car is full of loud music, perfume, and cigarette and dope smoke. Coughing, Parvez waves his hand to try and clear the air. The Prostitutes exchange cosmetics and look in mirrors.

> PARVEZ
> They're the top pillars of the whole community.

> MARGOT
> (*laughing*)
> Pillocks, more like.

> PARVEZ
> Don't drop the food.

Margot has her fingers in the dall.

> Margot, I am observing naughty fingers! Keep them for nimble uses later.

PROSTITUTE

Nimble uses!

MARGOT

So what's going on with you and Bettina?

PROSTITUTE I

Yeah.

PARVEZ

What has she told you?

PROSTITUTE

She won't tell us nothing.

PROSTITUTE 2

That's how we know it's serious!

PARVEZ

You silly girls imagine romances everywhere.
(*pause*)
What makes you think she likes me?

PROSTITUTE

She doesn't!

PARVEZ

What?

MARGOT
(*leans forward and whispers*)
But when she mentions you – she smiles a little bit.

Tears spring into Parvez's eyes.

PROSTITUTE 2

You're not like your son, then.

PROSTITUTE I

That lad and his people look at you like scum and frighten the
punters.

PARVEZ

What do they say?

PROSTITUTE

Abuse.

PROSTITUTE 2

A little one was beaten up.

PROSTITUTE

The dirty bastards carried her up to the moors and did her all
over. She was only fifteen. No one touches me!

PROSTITUTE I

Everyone touches you!

PROSTITUTE

Shut it!

PARVEZ
(*interrupting*)

How many times has my boy been there?

MARGOT

A few.

PARVEZ

I apologize for his behaviour. He's got many problems.

MARGOT

Why's he taking it out on us?

Parvez hangs his head.

EXT. OUTSIDE MILL – NIGHT

*The German stands waiting at the door, smoking a cigar. He walks
down and kisses the Girls as Parvez drops them off. Rashid's cab turns
up with another two Girls inside.*

GERMAN

Welcome, delicious tarts. Everything is ready but you!

CUT TO:

Come, little man, we are all thirsty and everyone is standing
still! Bring the drink!

As Parvez goes to the boot of his cab, the German kicks him up the arse and laughs. Parvez slips and falls, before getting up, and wiping his muddy ripped trousers.

PARVEZ

Please, don't ever do that to me, sir!

Angrily he goes towards the German, who grabs and restrains him.

INT. INSIDE MILL NIGHT

A group of Businessmen, a couple of Sikhs among them, are standing around in a cluster. Bettina is chatting to some of them. They perk up when Schitz leads the Girls into the room.

GERMAN

This way, gentlemen, for entertainment.

The Girls and the Businessmen eye each other up. Parvez and Rashid in the meantime bring in the crates of drink and the food.

INT. MILL NIGHT

The party is in full swing. Two of the Girls are stripping. Some of the Men are yelling encouragement. Other Men and Girls lie on couches. Bettina stands with Schitz.

The two Strippers start trying to undress the Men. One Sikh Businessman has his shirt off and trousers down. Another Man is resisting, as the Stripper sits on his chest and tries pulling his shirt off.

The unselfconscious Women seem to attack the Men, pulling at them, humiliating them.

Parvez, frantically pouring drinks and handing them to people, looks on. He and Bettina talk during all this. (This conversation should be broken up.)

BETTINA

The religious man still sleeps in your house?

PARVEZ

Until late in the morning when Farid brings his breakfast. He's so comfortable perhaps he will stay for ten years.

GERMAN
(*interrupts*)

Come along, big girl. You are wearing too many clothes, as
usual.

PARVEZ

The boys gather up and never stop talking about good and
bad, or God says do this or that, or burn in hell, or celebrate
in Paradise.
(*pause*)
Sandra, I am tired of being instructed, as if I am a fool or a
bad man without my own mind.
(*pause*)
You're right, they thirst for something. But why is there so
much violence and hatred there?
(*pause*)
It is true that Farid must go his own way. It must be
inevitable, with the children. If life for the parents isn't to
end, there must be . . . other interests.

CUT TO:

*A drunk Bettina goes over to Parvez, and kisses his face. Rashid
gesticulates at the wild scenes which have become a fracas. Parvez
shrugs.*

CUT TO:

*Bettina and Parvez standing with their arms around each other: she
whispers in his ear, he laughs. They start doing a little improvised dance
together.*

EXT. OUTSIDE THE MILL – NIGHT

*Parvez is paying the women from a fat wad. They wait in a line,
shivering in their skimpy clothes. Cold; raining; silent. The German sits
in a car watching.*

*Rashid leans against his car, watching scornfully. Bettina watches from
a distance.*

RASHID
(*in Urdu, subtitled*)
Money from immorality.

PARVEZ
(*in Urdu, subtitled*)
Is it wrong to help someone out?

RASHID
(*in Urdu, subtitled*)
Funny how it's whores and not your own kind. And you living with the Maulvi in your very own house.

Parvez suddenly loses his temper.

PARVEZ
(*in Urdu, subtitled*)
What right do you have to judge me, or these women? Come near me and I'll swipe you with the bat!

Rashid slinks off, cursing.

Good show, girls.

MARGOT
Ta very much for the work.

The German, sitting in a car, indicates to Bettina.

GERMAN
Come along, my love, back to the hotel.

Bettina looks at him. Looks at Parvez.

BETTINA
I am going with this one.

GERMAN
He can't afford your prices.

Bettina shakes her head at him. The German crooks his finger at another girl.

I'll have to make do with you!
(*to Parvez*)
She is hard to satisfy, little man!

INT. BETTINA'S BEDROOM

Bettina, exhausted, lies naked in the bed. She and Parvez have made love. Parvez, beside the bed, has almost finished putting his clothes on. He strokes and kisses her face. Bettina swoons.

BETTINA

I love you looking after me.

She pulls him by the hand.

Lie on top of me for a little while.

PARVEZ

I must go.

BETTINA

I want to hold you. Please.

He does so. Their faces together.

Oh man, I'm so tired.

PARVEZ

Sandra.

Parvez starts to move.

Bettina grabs him and pins him to the bed.

BETTINA

Now you must stay.

PARVEZ

I wish I could.

(*beat*)

Let me go.

BETTINA

No! Why should I?

Parvez struggles with her. They fight and kiss. He pulls away and gets to the door. Out in the hall he hears her voice behind him.

Never leave me! Never, never, never!

INT. PARVEZ'S BEDROOM – NIGHT

Minoo lies in bed. Parvez undresses.

> PARVEZ
> I'm bloody pleased to be back.

> MINOO
> Again you're muddy.

> PARVEZ
> This Schitz is getting my full value.

He indicates some money that he put on his bedside table.

> Here. Today I received a nice tip.

She takes the money. He watches her put it under her pillow.

> PARVEZ
> What will you do with it?

> MINOO
> Put it away for a better time.

PARVEZ

You know I want to take you to that place I saw. Can't we go on Sunday?

MINOO

It is the first time you have asked me to go out, and I am going to be too busy.

PARVEZ

Doing what?

MINOO

Looking after some things.

CUT TO:

They lie at each side of the bed. She turns off the light.

INT. PARVEZ'S HOUSE. HALL – MORNING

Parvez is picking the mail off the mat.

He seems very weary, emotionally and physically exhausted.

Downstairs a young Asian Kid is talking on a portable phone in the hall. Another Kid is with him. Parvez slides, with difficulty, around them.

The house seems full of people. As we follow him through the house we see someone yelling into a mobile phone; others are talking frantically; someone is making placards.

INT. PARVEZ'S HOUSE. LIVING ROOM – MORNING

He looks into the living room where the Maulvi is giving instructions to his young Deputies.

INT. PARVEZ'S HOUSE. KITCHEN – MORNING

PARVEZ

Minoo.

He opens the kitchen door. Inside he finds young women in the hijab cooking for the troops outside, someone else washing up. Meanwhile Minoo, in a comfortable chair, with her feet up, chats to the women, enjoying their company, and the hustle and bustle.

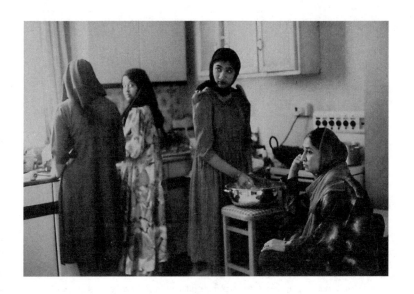

Parvez stands outside the door, not knowing what to do with himself.

PARVEZ

You boys are busy, eh?

LAD

Community spirit.

PARVEZ

Haven't I seen you?

LAD

Rashid's young brother – he works with you.

INT. PARVEZ'S HOUSE. LIVING ROOM – MORNING

In the living room Farid's young Friends are making placards and preparing for today's demonstration. Opening the mail which consists mainly of bills, Parvez surveys the scene.

The Maulvi goes to Parvez.

MAULVI

One word please.

The Maulvi and Parvez are alone in Parvez's cubby hole.

> MAULVI

I am in need of some legal advices.

Pause. He looks up to see that three of Farid's companions are standing outside the door. The Maulvi indicates for one of them to close the door.

My work is here. I will stay.

> PARVEZ

And bring your family?

> MAULVI

You knew that?

> PARVEZ

You are so patriotic about Pakistan. It is always a sign of imminent departure.

> MAULVI

Can you help me? In our own country we are treated badly, and everywhere else we are what? Pakis.
> (*pause*)

The point is . . .

The Maulvi drones on interminably while Parvez studies the phone bill which is for more than £500. Stunned, he immediately examines the rest of the mail. All of the bills are inordinately high; there is a threatening letter from the bank.

There are many who reject the teaching, they close their minds and choose atheism, thinking that bread is all that men need to live by, and that the sky is empty, but right conduct is possible provided the preacher warns and advises that in the military-industrial state the greatness of God's guidance is essential in guaranteeing repentance . . . Loss of faith in all areas is common here, but poor preachers can move mountains, that is all I am here to inform the masses of . . .

Parvez stares at the burbling Maulvi.

INT. PARVEZ'S HOUSE. HALL — MORNING

In the hall Parvez leans against the wall in a state of virtual collapse.

> PARVEZ
> (*calls*)

Farid!

Minoo hurries towards him. Farid comes out of the front room

> MINOO

What's the matter?

> PARVEZ

Now I will never pay off mortgage!

> MINOO

I will get a glass of water!

Farid holds on to Parvez's arm, looking at the bills.

> PARVEZ

I can't breathe!

> FARID

Papa! A few pounds is worth it for what we are trying to achieve. The house price will increase once the tarts have gone.

> PARVEZ

One of the little ones was beaten up on the moors.

> FARID

Propaganda. Why are you taking their side?

> PARVEZ

Your great long-beard friend wants to stay in this immoral country. Knowing of my Fingerhut connections he asked me to help him with the immigration.

Farid looks at his father and turns away.

Minoo has opened the front door and let several young men into the house, who look at Parvez, yelling.

Farid turns away to greet the visitors.

Parvez puts his head in his hands.

Minoo holds the telephone receiver.

> MINOO
>
> The German is calling you.

EXT. OUTSIDE PARVEZ'S HOUSE – DAY

As Parvez gets into his car and drives away, the Maulvi, Farid, and their companions are leaving the house with banners and placards.

INT. FIZZY'S RESTAURANT – DAY

Fizzy is sitting in the restaurant doing his paperwork. (Perhaps there is a screen around his table.) He looks up as Parvez goes slowly towards him. Seeing Parvez's expression he becomes concerned.

CUT TO:

They sit across the table, Fizzy examining the bills as Parvez points out their worst features.

> PARVEZ
>
> Can you believe it?

> FIZZY
>
> They say you have lost control of him.

> PARVEZ
> (*impatiently*)
>
> The boy will grow less zealous when he improves overall.

> FIZZY
>
> Everyone says it was him, personally, who invited this man into your house. They're agitated, yaar, and complaining to me like mad.

> PARVEZ
>
> If he doesn't bugger off I'll report him to immigration authorities.
> (*trying to change the subject*)
> Fizzy, friend . . . I've never come to you before.

Fizzy extracts his chequebook with a flourish and begins to write a cheque.

FIZZY

Yes, yes, shut up. But I haven't signed.

(beat)

You came with that tart here. The community is small but the big mouths say you two are doing something together.

PARVEZ

All the drivers are up to it – everyone in England full-time in fact.

FIZZY

You have never been a cheap man. But she –

PARVEZ

Even you, friend, are divorced, let me –

FIZZY

She is an old whore that even a taxi-driver could afford! Everybody fucks her – thousands of dicks.

III

PARVEZ

Shut up!

(*And adds much extra abuse, in Urdu*)

FIZZY

Perhaps it is lucky that your new lodger is sending them away. You've always been naïve, Parvez.

PARVEZ

Naïve?

FIZZY

Minoo's parents paid my fare to England! I came to your wedding!

PARVEZ

I know, I know –

FIZZY

You will stop seeing the woman. Otherwise –

He stops writing the cheque and looks at Parvez. Parvez looks back at him. He begins to boil; he loses his temper.

PARVEZ

Stick it in your backside! I won't beg, Fizzy!

FIZZY

You don't like this woman, do you? So you do. I can tell.

PARVEZ

What else is there for me, yaar, but sitting behind the wheel without tenderness? That's it for me, is it, until I drop dead, and not another human touch.

Parvez starts to sob.

You are too certain of what everyone else should do! Minoo has never given me satisfaction. Who am I satisfying? You? Go to hell!

He gets up and walks out.

EXT. STREET – DAY

Parvez is striding down the street towards his car. We see Fizzy hurrying behind him.

FIZZY

Here, here!

Fizzy hands Parvez the cheque.

Parvez turns and, in front of Fizzy, rips up the cheque. The bits of paper scatter in the wind.

INT./EXT. PARVEZ'S TAXI – DAY

Parvez is taking the German to the airport.

GERMAN

At last I'm going home, little man. The women are the one good thing about this town.

Parvez is taking another route and loses his way. He notices the traffic is bad, and there are a lot of people heading in one direction.

PARVEZ
(*mutters*)

What the hell is all this? What are these bloody people doing now?

GERMAN

Look out! Where are you going man! I'll miss my flight!

PARVEZ
(*driving in another direction*)

Sir, special short cut.

GERMAN

What are they doing here! We don't have time . . . Turn around now . . . don't get out!

INT./EXT. SEEDY STREET – DAY

Parvez takes a turn and there, on the street, is the anti-prostitutes demonstration. People are waving banners, and shouting. The women stand in their places swearing, cursing, brandishing fists. The atmosphere is tense.

The German is first exasperated, then incredulous.

Parvez tries to drive through the crowd beeping his horn, but can't make any progress.

Some of the Crowd start hammering on the roof and the few Police that are there shout at Parvez to get his taxi away. But the cab is stuck, unable to move forward or back and all Parvez can do is sit there in a daze.

Then Parvez catches sight through the mêlee *of the Maulvi with Farid next to him.*

Next to them is one of the Drivers – Rashid – and all of them are exchanging insults with a group of Prostitutes among whom, at the back, is Bettina.

At the head of the Prostitutes is the Addict Prostitute who points at Rashid and shouts out that he was fucking her only last week and makes derogatory remarks about the size of his dick, etc.

Furious, Rashid, breaking rank, races forward and strikes the Addict, knocking her to the floor. Immediately the other Prostitutes set upon him and all hell breaks loose as the demonstrators also join in.

To the German's horror, Parvez gets out of the cab. He is trying desperately to locate Bettina.

Suddenly she finds herself facing Farid and stops short. The boy looks at her for a moment then, with the Maulvi's eye on him, spits in her face.

Incensed, Parvez barges his way through the crowd until he gets to her.

He wipes her face with his handkerchief.

He looks around for Farid. When he sees him, he grabs him by the scruff of his neck and drags him back towards the cab. Reaching it, he sees that some of the crowd are venting their anger on it, rocking it violently from side to side with the terrified German still inside.

Parvez shoves the demonstrators away before throwing his son into the

front passenger seat. When the German screams and swears at Parvez for leaving him Parvez reaches for his cricket bat and, brandishes it.

PARVEZ

Get out of my car! Out!

As the hapless German tries to take himself and his luggage out of harm's way Parvez drives off, the crowd parting in front of his accelerating cab.

INT. PARVEZ'S HOUSE

A distraught Minoo watched Parvez drag Farid upstairs to his bedroom. Hurling the boy into the room Parvez regards the Maulvi's possessions with disgust.

Behind them Minoo pushes at the door. Parvez bangs it shut and sticks a chair under the handle.

PARVEZ

Get this crap out!

Farid hesitates. Parvez starts to throw the Maulvi's clothes, toilet articles and learned books into his suitcase.

FARID

No!

PARVEZ

He could be Jesus Christ himself, but he is leaving!

Farid tries to stop him by pulling the things from Parvez's hands. Parvez pulls them back and pushes his son away.

FARID

If you shame me, I am going away too! Put in my things!

PARVEZ
(*staring at Farid*)

All right! I won't stand for the extremity of anti-democratic and anti-Jewish rubbish! And he eats too much!

FARID

Only the corrupt would say it is extreme to want goodness!

PARVEZ

But there is nothing of God in spitting on a woman's face!
This cannot be the way for us to take!

FARID
(*slyly*)
Why are you so interested in dirty whores? Is it because –

*Behind them Minoo is pushing at the door. She can see and hear
through the gap.*

PARVEZ

What nonsense is this?

FARID
You do it to one of them, don't you? It's been going on for –

PARVEZ

Farid!

FARID

Answer!

PARVEZ
You listen to the gossip of fools?

FARID
They know you better than we do!

PARVEZ
Would they be drivers if they weren't ignorant fools? We drive
the women and they pay us.

FARID
It is all around, everyone says so . . . it makes me feel sick to
have such a father! I never thought you were such a man!
. . . You are a pimp who organizes sexual parties!

*Parvez grabs him and starts to hit him around the head. Farid falls
backwards. Parvez is so angry he grabs him again and continues to
whack him.*

You call me fanatic, dirty man, but who is the fanatic now?

Father and son struggle desperately.

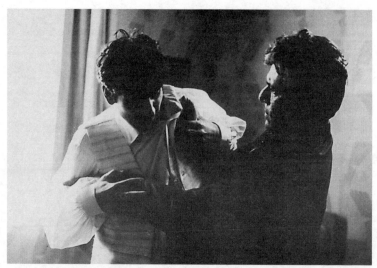

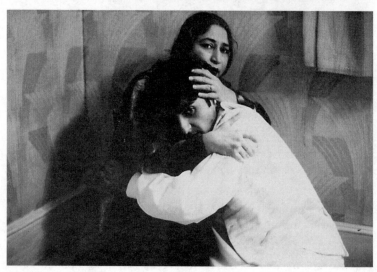

Minoo has broken into the room.

> **MINOO**
> You have killed him!

> **PARVEZ**
> He will recover, I am afraid.

> **MINOO**
> These minutes have made me into an old woman.

Minoo goes to Farid and helps him up, kissing and holding him.

Parvez looks at them.

INT. HOUSE – DAY

An agitated, disturbed and regretful Parvez is walking around the house with a glass in his hand.

He smashes an unused placard over his knee and throws it in the bin.

Minoo comes in.

> **MINOO**
> Papu, please, don't let him go.

> **PARVEZ**
> Yes, it will be only us.

> **MINOO**
> I will be here alone, like the English women, waiting to die.

> **PARVEZ**
> He will do what he wants.
> (*beat*)
> Minoo, just tell me, what can I do to make you happy? If you just tell me once, then I will know for good!

> **MINOO**
> Is it true – you have a friendship with one of those women?

> **PARVEZ**
> Yes, a friendship.

MINOO

Filthy selfish man!

PARVEZ

Friendship is . . . good, Minoo. I think it can be found . . . in the funniest places. Other people can be useful, and nice.

MINOO

All this time I stayed here to serve you, and you were out, laughing with low-class people! What a fool I've been made into! What a waste.

He watches her howling. He considers going to comfort her, but is unable to do so. He turns away.

Papu.

He turns. She throws a glass at his head.

Parvez looks up and sees Farid standing at the door with his bag. Minoo turns and sees too.

The front door bangs.

Go to him! Go!

EXT. STREET – DAY

Parvez, in his taxi, drives along the street beside Farid, who is carrying his suitcases.

PARVEZ

Remember two things. There are many ways of being a good man. And I will be at home. Will you come to see me?

Parvez stops and watches him go. Out of the shadows several of Farid's companions emerge, waiting for him.

Parvez watches the boy go.

INT. THE BEDROOM – DAY

Minoo is going through her cupboards, sorting her clothes out. Suitcases on the bed.

PARVEZ

What is this?

MINOO

I will see everyone who loves me, my brothers and sisters and all! Come, Papu, I am begging you, husband.

PARVEZ

There is nothing there for me.

MINOO

You are not Prime Minister. They require drivers –

PARVEZ

You can't go home, Minoo. It isn't like that now. This is our home.

MINOO

I hate this dirty place! The men brought us here and then left us alone!

PARVEZ

Oh you make me ashamed, so ashamed! But I have done nothing wrong, I know I haven't.

MINOO

Oh yes, one unforgivable thing.

He looks at her.

Put self before family.

PARVEZ

Oh God, yes. The first time! But not the last!

MINOO

Is it because of her that you won't come? Yes, yes.

PARVEZ
(*shaking his head*)
Perhaps one day the boy will tire of his moral exertions and will need me. I will wait. You will come home?

MINOO

Do you want me to?

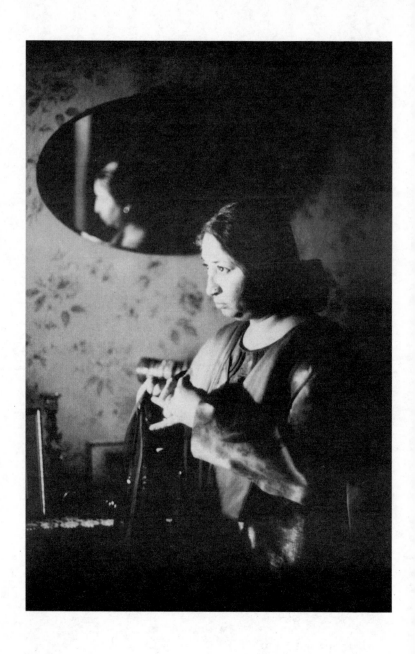

PARVEZ

If you want to.

MINOO

I will then.

Parvez with his head in his hands.

PARVEZ

Otherwise I will come to get you. It is too late now for us to be parted for good.

MINOO

No it is not. I can tell you have lost your feeling for me.

EXT. COUNTRYSIDE – DAY

Bettina and Parvez are walking through a wood with some distance between them. She picks up leaves and pieces of tree bark.

PARVEZ

I have managed to destroy everything. I have never felt worse . . . or better.

CUT TO:

Another part of the wood.

BETTINA

Can't we leave?

PARVEZ

Where?

BETTINA

I thought . . . India. Parvez, a few weeks. You can show me the good places. We can live cheaply, everybody says.

PARVEZ

That's a young people's thing, yaar.

BETTINA

Why have you never been back?

PARVEZ

No time, no money –

123

BETTINA

Come away. It's a chance! Otherwise . . . what will we do but the same thing every day!

PARVEZ

You put such ideas in my head!

BETTINA

Good. Good.

She holds him. They kiss.

PARVEZ

What do you want?

BETTINA

More than I've ever had before.

Pause. He looks at her questioningly.

Your face, your hands, you, all of you, you.

INT. PARVEZ'S HOUSE – NIGHT

Parvez comes into the darkened house. Everyone has gone. It is eerily silent. He puts the lights on.

*Still wearing his coat, he pushes the doors of the various rooms –
kitchen, bedroom, Farid's room – putting on the lights as he walks
through the empty place.*

*Finally he sits down, alone, and pours himself a drink. He holds the
glass up, swirls the liquid around, and drinks.*

*He puts on his favourite Louis Armstrong (or similar) record. Music fills
the house. He dances.*

EXT. PARVEZ'S HOUSE – NIGHT

*Parvez's house, its windows blazing with light in the middle of a dark
terrace.*

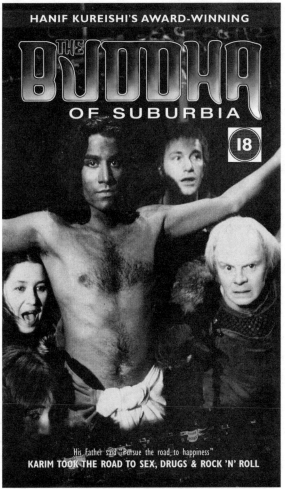